CAUGHT BY LOVE

The Marquis walked deep into the stable. "Where are you?"

"I am . . . here," Cara replied.

He realized that she had climbed up into the hayrack. He walked to stand immediately below her and put up his arms. "I will not let you fall."

She put one leg over the side and leaned over, her arms going out towards him to hold onto his shoulders, then she fell into his arms. He felt her arms go around his neck, and she said in a terrified whisper:

"They are . . . going to . . . kill you! Tomorrow night!"

He could feel her heart beating frantically against his. His arms tightened around her. "How could you come here? How could you do anything so incredibly . . ." He stopped.

Then, as he knew there was no need for words, his lips found hers and he kissed her. As he did so he knew that he was in love . . .

Bantam Books by Barbara Cartland
Ask your bookseller for the books you have missed

Caught by Love

Barbara Cartland

BANTAM BOOKS
TORONTO · NEW YORK · LONDON · SYDNEY

CAUGHT BY LOVE
A Bantam Book / September 1982

ISBN 0-553-22611-8

Published simultaneously in the United States and Canada

Bantam Books are published by Bantam Books, Inc. Its trademark,
consisting of the words "Bantam Books" and the portrayal of a
rooster, is Registered in U.S. Patent and Trademark Office and in
other countries. Marca Registrada. Bantam Books, Inc., 666 Fifth
Avenue, New York, New York 10103.

PRINTED IN THE UNITED STATES OF AMERICA

H   0 9 8 7 6 5 4 3 2 1

Author's Note

The Cato Street Conspiracy was exactly as I have described it. Thistlewood, the renegade gentleman who had been in prison, planned to murder the entire Cabinet when they were dining at Lord Harrowby's home at 44 Grosvenor Square on Fedruary 23, 1820.

Lord Harrowby was warned on the morning of the dinner-party. The Duke of Wellington warned the Prime Minister not to alter the arrangements, but other Members were not so eager to meet the assassins.

So the dinner was cancelled, although none of the members of Lord Harrowby's staff, including his French Chef, were told.

One of Thistlewood's spies, hiding in the Square, saw guests arriving for a dinner-party two doors away, at the home of the Archbishop of York, and thought they were the Cabinet arriving at Lord Harrowby's.

He reported back to Cato Street that all was well, then just as the conspirators were ready to set out, a party of Bow Street Officers appeared at the foot of a loft-ladder.

Thistlewood killed their leader with a sword. Someone snuffed the candles, and a terrible fight took place, during which he escaped.

In the middle of it, Captain Fitzclarence arrived with a troop of Goldstream Guards. He was late, as he had lost his way, but the soldiers arrested nine of the criminals, including Archie Ings, the butcher, a Negro, a bootmaker, and a cabinet-maker. Thistlewood was caught the next day.

Five of the conspirators, including Thistlewood and Ings, were ordered to be hanged, and the rest were transported to Australia.

A crowd of thousands watched the hanging outside Newgate Prison.

Caught by Love

Chapter One
1820

The Marquis of Broome stifled a yawn.

He was finding the hot, airless atmosphere of Carlton House more intolerable than usual and he wondered how soon he would be able to leave.

Although he admired the Prince Regent for quite a number of reasons, he was growing increasingly bored with the endless parties that succeeded one another and about which there was little variety.

The only thing that ever changed was the Regent's heart. At the moment, the Marquis thought that Lady Hertford was on her way out and that her place as Royal Favourite would doubtless be taken very shortly by the Marchioness of Conyingham.

Whichever large, fat, elderly woman it might be, he thought, her conversation would be very much the same, and she would betray her ignorance of the feeling in the country every time she opened her mouth.

One thing which the Marquis really enjoyed at Carlton House was the collection of paintings, to which the Regent added almost weekly, together with the furniture, the statues, and the objets d'art which made the Royal Residence look more and more like a Museum.

He yawned again, and this time one of his friends, Lord Hansketh, who was passing, stopped to say:

"Are you bored, Ivo, or merely tired from your excesses of last night?"

"Bored!" the Marquis replied briefly.

"I thought you chose the pick of the bunch," Henry Hansketh continued. "I found my 'charmer' talked too much, and if there is one thing I find tiresome it is a yapping woman as the dawn breaks."

The Marquis did not reply, and his friend remembered that it was one of his rules never to discuss the women in whom he was interested, whether they were Ladies of Quality or "bits o' muslin."

"I should think 'Prinny' will retire soon," he said, to change the subject. "It is one blessing that as he has grown older he does not wish to stay up so late."

"I agree with you," the Marquis replied. "I remember times in the past when it was inevitable that the sun should be in the sky before the Prince of Wales struck his feathers."

Lord Hansketh laughed and repeated:

"'Struck his feathers!' I must remember that, Ivo. It is one of your better *bons mots!*"

"I will make you a present of it," the Marquis drawled. "You will doubtless use it anyway."

His friend grinned.

"Why not? You are always more witty than the rest of us, and it is therefore one thing we can steal from you with impunity."

However, the Marquis was not listening. He saw that the Prince Regent was offering his arm to Lady Hertford, which meant that he was getting ready to escort her from the Chinese Drawing-Room.

He calculated that with any luck he would be able to leave Carlton House in the next ten minutes.

As if his intention had transmitted itself, Lord Hansketh said:

"What is your next appointment, Ivo? I wonder if I can guess who will be waiting for you."

"You can save your more odious innuendoes for somebody else," the Marquis replied. "As it happens, as soon as I leave here I am driving to Broome."

"At this time of night?" Henry Hansketh exclaimed.

The Marquis nodded.

"I have a horse I am particularly eager to try out before the Steeple-Chase next Saturday."

"Which of course you intend to win!"

"That depends on how good this particular stallion is."

There was silence for a moment. Then Lord Hansketh exclaimed:

"Of course! I know what you are talking about. You bought quite a number of animals at poor D'Arcy's sale, and I suppose this is one of them."

"You suppose right," the Marquis said drily. "And as it happens I was very annoyed when D'Arcy purchased *Agamemnon* at Tattersall's one day when I was unable to be there."

"*Agamemnon!*" Lord Hansketh repeated. "I remember the animal! A magnificent beast! It caused a commotion when it took at least three men to bring him into the ring."

He saw a faint smile on the Marquis's lips before he said:

"I was told how wild he was, and although I offered to buy him from D'Arcy, he was intent on keeping him so that he could force up the price. But he never had a chance of controlling the animal himself."

"Which of course you will be able to do easily!" Henry Hansketh said mockingly.

"It is what I intend to do," the Marquis answered quietly.

He spoke with a self-assurance and confidence in his own ability, which was characteristic.

An extremely handsome man, he was taller than most other men in the room, and there was not an ounce of superfluous flesh on his slim, athletic body.

The Marquis of Broome was greatly admired for his successes in the sporting world. In fact, he had a public following and was cheered on every race-course.

At the same time, those who considered themselves his friends found him unpredictable and in many ways an enigma.

Although every beautiful woman was prepared to lay her heart at his feet, he was known to be so fastidious about those in whom he showed an interest that he had earned the reputation of being heartless and often completely callous.

"He is cruel—cruel," one Beauty had sobbed to anyone who would listen.

This was strange, because the Marquis was violently opposed to any form of cruelty where sport was concerned.

He had been instrumental in making bull-baiting taboo in the Fashionable World and had been known to thrash a man with his own whip if he saw him ill-treating a horse.

But the tears of a woman left the Marquis unmoved, however pathetic she might appear or however lovely she looked when she was weeping.

As was fashionable, the Marquis like all his contemporaries regularly had a "Fair Cyprian" under his protection.

This was invariably an "Incomparable" who was pursued by the Bucks and Beaux of St. James's Street, and whom he carried off under their noses, much to their chagrin and jealousy.

"If you ask me," Lord Hansketh had said at White's Club confidentially to a friend, "I do not believe Broome has the slightest interest in the women he instals in his house in Chelsea and covers with diamonds, except that it infuriates all of us who are unable to compete when the stakes are so high."

"If you are telling me that Broome did not really want Linette, I think I shall blow a piece of lead through him," replied the man to whom he was talking.

Henry Hansketh laughed.

"You have as much chance of doing that, Charlie, as flying over the moon. Have you forgotten how quick Ivo is with a pistol? Nobody has ever been known to win a duel against him yet."

"Damn him! Why does he always pass the winning-post first, whether it is with horses or women?"

Henry Hansketh laughed again.

"You are envious, that is what is wrong with you. But because I am very fond of Ivo, I realise he is not really a happy man."

"Not happy?" Charlie exclaimed incredulously. "Of course he is! How could he not be happy with all that wealth and so many possessions that I have ceased to count them?"

"I still think Ivo is missing something in life," Henry Hansketh persisted.

"And what is that?" Charlie asked aggressively.

Lord Hansketh did not reply.

As he had driven home from White's to his lodgings in Half-Moon Street he was thinking that in all the years he had been a close friend of the Marquis, he had never known him to fall in love.

They had been quite young men when they had first served in Wellington's Army, and there Ivo, who had not yet inherited his father's Marquisate, had been not only the best-looking Officer in the Life Guards but also the most dashing, the bravest, and undoubtedly the most admired.

When he and Henry were off duty they had enjoyed the company of attractive women, whether they were of the *Beau Monde* or were "Ladies of the Town."

But while their friends sighed over, pursued, and captured the women of their fancy, Ivo remained completely self-sufficient, and if he ever yearned after a woman, his closest friends were not aware of it.

But women certainly yearned after him, and Lord Hansketh, who was continually with the Marquis, was well aware of the numerous scented notes that arrived from first thing in the morning until last thing at night at his house in Berkeley Square.

Whether he opened and read them and whether he ever replied remained a mystery, but they were undoubtedly there.

Yet it was true to say that the gossips found it hard in their endless chatter to find anything about the Marquis's love-life which indicated marriage.

Henry Hansketh was at this moment wondering if the Marquis was going to Broome alone or whether he would suggest that he should go with him.

If there was one thing he really enjoyed, it was riding the Marquis's superlative horses. Moreover, they had been friends for so long that they always had a great deal to discuss, and the hours they spent together were not only intellectually enjoyable but inevitably amusing.

Then Henry Hansketh remembered that unfortunately he had promised the Regent he would be in attendance tomorrow morning when he visited Buckingham Palace to enquire after the health of the King.

His Majesty was deteriorating day by day, and now in his eighty-second year he was greatly emaciated.

Because the eternal waiting depressed the Regent, he usually asked somebody he trusted and of whom he was fond to accompany him on his calls of duty.

"When will you be back?" Lord Hansketh asked now.

The Marquis, who was watching the Regent making a number of somewhat prolonged farewells at the end of the Drawing-Room, replied:

"I am not sure. Wednesday, or perhaps Thursday."

"If you have not returned by then, I shall come and join you," Lord Hansketh said.

"That will certainly encourage me to stay in the country," the Marquis answered. "I cannot think why anybody wants to be in London when there is hunting to be enjoyed."

"I agree with you. We should keep all this bowing and knee-bending until after the hunting-season is over."

"The one blessing is that the King is supposed to be really dying this time. 'Prinny' is talking of cancelling his parties, and that should let us off the hook for a little while."

"You have cheered me up," Henry Hansketh replied. "At the same time, I cannot help suspecting that this filial affection will not last for long."

The Marquis did not reply, but there was an expression in his eyes which was more eloquent than words, and Henry Hansketh was quite certain that while he himself would find it impossible to escape any of the Carlton House parties, the Marquis would somehow manage it.

The Regent was now definitely moving towards the door, while all the ladies as he passed sank down into a deep curtsey and the gentlemen bowed their heads from the neck.

Fat, florid, and yet with an indefinable charm which no-one could deny, the Prince, with Lady Hertford clinging to his arm, finally disappeared from sight, and the Marquis exclaimed:

"Now I can go! Can I give you a lift, Henry?"

"No, thank you," his friend replied. "I have two or three people to talk to before I leave. Do not stay at Broome longer than you have to. All the same, I envy you the fresh air, and of course the battle you will enjoy with *Agamemnon*."

The faint twist on the Marquis's lips told his friend that that was what he was looking forward to.

"I think it would be best," the Marquis said after a slight pause, "if you definitely joined me on Thursday evening or Friday. Then, however much we are needed here, we need not return until Monday."

"All right, Ivo," Henry Hansketh agreed. "I had promised to dine with a certain very attractive lady on Friday night, but I will make my apologies and join you at Broome."

The Marquis did not wait to hear his friend's acceptance, taking it for granted, and was already walking quickly from the Chinese Drawing-Room, having avoided with some dexterity the Princess de Lieven, wife of the Russian Ambassador.

She was an acknowledged wit and had also pursued the Marquis for some time without gaining her objective.

He hurried down the graceful double staircase, which had amazed those who saw it when the house was first finished, and into the splendid Hall decorated with Ionic columns of brown Siena marble.

A flunkey placed a fur-lined cape over his shoulders, then he walked out through the front door under the high Corinthian portico, where Linkman immediately appeared and called out:

"The carriage of the Most Noble Marquis of Broome!"

The Marquis had already instructed his servants that he would be leaving as early as possible, and as it drew up a few seconds later where he was waiting, all eyes were on the six perfectly matched and superbly bred jet-black stallions.

The chariot they were drawing had only recently been delivered from the carriage-maker and was so light and so well sprung that it appeared as if its brightly painted yellow wheels hardly touched the ground.

The Marquis stepped into it, the footman put a sable rug over his black satin knee-breeches; then, having shut the door, which was emblazoned with the

Broome coat-of-arms, the man sprang up onto the box as the horses were already moving.

One thing the Marquis particularly disliked was taking a long time on any journey.

While he expected his coachmen to drive with the expertise he had himself, he also demanded a speed which usually left any passengers who were with him sitting tense on the edge of their seats and wondering if they would ever reach their destination alive.

The Marquis had no such qualms, unlike many Corinthians who disliked being driven, being such expert hands with the reins themselves, for he had complete trust in his coachmen, who had all been with him for many years.

As soon as the horses moved out of the traffic in Pall Mall into St. James's Street, and then into Piccadilly, the Marquis leant back against the well-padded seat of the chariot, lifted his silk-stockinged legs, and put his feet on the opposite seat.

It was heavily padded, and it needed to be, because it was not only a seat but also a safe with a very special lock in which valuables were carried on long journeys.

Highwaymen, if they were intrepid enough to bring the carriage to a halt, were unaware of its existence.

The Marquis had in fact designed this particular safe himself, making sure that it was deep and wide enough to hold all the valuables he might wish to carry with him. At the same time, it was comfortable if used as a seat by his guests.

However, at the moment he was thinking not of his chariot but of the pleasure he would derive tomorrow when he rode *Agamemnon* for the first time.

He was looking forward to his struggle with a horse which he knew would demand all his expertise as an outstanding rider to bring it under control.

He was also, as Lord Hansketh had surmised, slightly fatigued.

It took a great deal to tire the Marquis, but he had

been out extremely late the night before and for several previous nights in succession.

But however late he was, it never prevented him when he was in London from riding very early in the Park before the presence of other riders made it difficult to exercise either himself or the horse he was riding in the way he wished.

What was more, this morning after breakfast he had gone to Wimbledon to watch a mill between two pugilists, to one of whom he had given his patronage, and who not unexpectedly had won the contest.

After this he had had luncheon with the Prime Minister and a Member of the Cabinet, when they had discussed certain problems in which the Marquis was particularly interested.

He was concerned with the outbreaks of violence, revolutionary behaviour, and fierce threats against the social order which had been such a feature of the year 1815 and which seemed to be beginning again.

A number of the more optimistic Statesmen thought this an exaggeration of the position.

But Lord Sidmouth had supported the Marquis, saying he had little doubt that "the clouds in the North would soon burst," and as he had said to the Lord Chancellor, Lord Elton, he wished he could convince himself of the "sufficiency of the means, either by law or force, to curb the spirit of revolt."

Very few of the Marquis's social friends, except for Lord Hansketh, had any idea how at such private meetings his opinions were listened to with interest and his ideas noted.

"Something has to be done, and done quickly!" he told himself now. "Otherwise we shall undoubtedly have trouble, because reform is long overdue."

He started to enumerate to himself the measures he would bring in if he were Prime Minister.

By now his horses had carried him out from the suburbs into the open country and were travelling at a tremendous pace over roads that were dry after quite a long spell without rain and with only a mild frost at nights.

As the Marquis had known when he planned his journey, there was a full moon, and therefore the coachman did not have to rely on the inadequate lantern-light of the chariot.

He could see his way quite clearly beneath the Heavens ablaze with stars and the moonbeams that lit the land.

It would take, as the Marquis knew, less than two hours to reach Broome, which was situated in the Surrey hills.

He was almost asleep when he was alerted, not by any movement of the chariot but by the fact that for some reason he could not understand his feet were being pressed upwards.

At first he was just vaguely aware that they were rising. Then it crossed his mind that the lock of his safe could not have been closed properly.

This was something that annoyed him in that he expected perfection in everything round him.

Angrily he lifted his feet onto the floor, pushed aside the rug, and bent forward to feel if the lock was loose, indicating that it had not been fastened as it should have been.

Then to his astonishment the top of the seat rose even higher, and in the moonlight coming through the windows he realised that it was being lifted from the inside.

"What the Devil . . . ?" he began to say beneath his breath.

Then, going into action, he put his hand into the dark aperture beneath the raised cushion-top to clasp with fingers like steel what was beneath it.

There was a cry of pain, and the Marquis, feeling something warm and soft in his grasp, drew it out into the carriage.

To his astonishment, he found that what he held was a young boy who fell at his feet, exclaiming accusingly:

"You hurt . . . me!"

"Who are you and what are you doing here?" the Marquis demanded angrily.

"I was hiding."

The boy, sitting on the floor, was rubbing his neck with his hand as he spoke, and the Marquis could see that his head was covered with fair curls.

He was a very small boy, which accounted for the fact that he had been able to hide in the empty safe.

"I presume you were trying to steal something from me," the Marquis said harshly, "but we moved before you could escape."

The boy did not reply, but went on rubbing his neck, and after a moment the Marquis asked:

"What I want to know is how you knew there was a hiding-place beneath that seat, and how you opened it when it should have been locked."

Now the boy looked up at him and he saw that his face was small, with an oval forehead, a pointed chin, and eyes that appeared very large.

There was silence until the Marquis said:

"I am waiting for an answer, and I advise you to tell the truth before I hand you over to my servants to punish you as you undoubtedly deserve."

"I did not steal anything from you," the boy replied. "As I told you, I was hiding."

"From whom, and why in my carriage?"

"Because it is drawn by six horses."

The Marquis was suddenly aware that the boy's voice was cultured and unusually musical.

It was also surprising that he seemed not as frightened as he should have been, but was sitting quietly on the floor, his legs under him.

The Marquis saw now that he was wearing a short jacket, the type that he himself had worn when he was at

Eton, but instead of the conventional white collar he wore a dark silk scarf tied in a bow.

"I suppose you have some explanation for your behaviour," he said, "and I am certainly entitled to hear it."

"I was not doing anything wrong," the boy replied, "except taking a lift without asking your permission. Once you have carried me out of London I will disappear and you will not be bothered with me any further."

He paused before he went on:

"With any luck you would not have known of my existence, except that I was so cramped and it was so airless that I could not stand being cooped up any longer. I was afraid I might die of suffocation."

"It would have served you right if you had," the Marquis said grimly, "but I still want to know how you got into my coach in the first place and how you know of that particular hiding-place."

He knew the boy smiled before he replied:

"As it happens, my uncle, as a prevention against Highwaymen, has had exactly the same type of safe fitted into the travelling-chariot he has just purchased."

The Marquis stiffened.

"I do not believe it! It was my own invention, and the coach-builders assured me on their honour that there would be no replicas of it sold in any circumstances."

The boy laughed, and the Marquis thought it was a mocking sound.

"You must have a very trusting nature! Some men would sell the secrets of the Tower of London if you paid them enough money."

"Dammit, I will never give that firm another order!" the Marquis exclaimed.

"As a matter of fact, it was not the firm but one of their employees, whom they dismissed for taking bribes."

The Marquis's lips tightened and he said:

"I find what you have told me as reprehensible as the fact that you are here. Who are you and what is your name?"

"I do not have to answer that question," the boy retorted with unexpected dignity. "All I ask is that you will put me down in any town that you pass through before you reach your destination, and then forget that you have ever seen me."

"It seems a very strange request," the Marquis replied, "and I would like to know a little more about you before I agree to what you have asked me."

"There is no reason why you should be interested in me," the boy answered. "As I have already said, you would not have known I was here if I had not felt it so difficult to breathe that I thought I would faint."

"You are not fainting now," the Marquis said, "and I suggest you sit down in the seat opposite me, so that I can look at you, and tell me the truth about yourself."

The boy laughed, and the Marquis thought it was a very young, spontaneous sound.

"I doubt if you would believe me," he said, "but let me assure Your Lordship that it would be much better for you to remain in complete ignorance about me and the reason why I am accepting your hospitality for a short distance."

The way the boy spoke made the Marquis's lips twist slightly in amusement before he said:

"I presume you are running away from School or your Teachers! Let me tell you that it is not only a very unwise thing to do, but one that is likely to prove dangerous."

"That is my business!"

As the boy spoke he moved from the position in which he had remained ever since the Marquis had drawn him out from his hiding-place.

Rubbing one of his legs, which obviously hurt him, he sat down as the Marquis had instructed on the seat which was now closed and continued to rub his leg.

"If you are in pain," the Marquis said coldly, "you have nobody to blame but yourself."

"I know," the boy answered, "but I am suffering from 'pins and needles' as the blood comes back into my leg, and it is extremely unpleasant."

As he spoke he pulled his leg up so that his foot was on the seat on which he was sitting, and raised his trouser-leg to rub his ankle.

"It hurts!" he said. "It was so numb that I could not feel it at first."

"You will receive no sympathy from me," the Marquis replied, "and the sooner you return home, the better."

"I have no intention of doing that," the boy said positively, "and nothing you or anyone else can say will make me!"

The Marquis could not see very clearly even in the moonlight, but the boy's voice was not broken, and as he was small and his hands and his bones seemed delicate, the Marquis was sure he was very young.

"Now listen to me," he said in a different tone. "All boys at some time in their lives feel like running away from their family and their lessons. But you have no idea of the difficulties you will encounter in the world outside the security of your home. Go back and do not be a young idiot!"

"No!" the boy said defiantly.

"How long do you think you will last on your own with no money?" the Marquis enquired.

"I have quite a lot of money on me."

"Which no doubt will be stolen from you by the first tramp you meet! You will be lucky if he does not knock you about as well."

"You are trying to frighten me," the boy said, "but there is nothing you can say that can frighten me half so much as the cause of my running away."

"Suppose you tell me what it is?" the Marquis suggested.

"You would not believe me."

"How can you be sure of that? I have heard a lot of strange stories one way or another in my life, and if they seemed truthful and genuine I have always tried to help."

"Are you offering to help me?"

"I am."

There was silence. Then the boy, putting down his leg, said slowly:

"In a way I would like to trust you . . . but I think it would be a . . . mistake."

"For you or for me?" the Marquis enquired with a smile.

"For both of us, but especially for you. I can assure you that if you encumbered yourself with me, it is something you would undoubtedly regret. That is why, as soon as your horses stop, I am going to get out and you will never see me again."

"You cannot imagine how infuriating I shall find it if you leave me wondering who you are and what has happened to you," the Marquis said. "So now, my young friend, you must pay your way by revealing to me the story, whether it is true or false."

The boy gave an unexpected chuckle.

"You make me sound like Sheherazade."

"Sheherazade was a woman!"

There was silence. Then the Marquis said slowly:

"I think, unless I am mistaken, that I have found the answer to the first puzzle!"

For a moment he thought that the small figure opposite him was going to deny it. Then she asked:

"Was it so obvious? I thought if I cut my hair short nobody would ever guess I was not a boy."

"If I had seen you in the daylight I should have guessed sooner," the Marquis answered. "A boy's voice, even at the age you appear to be, would be deeper and certainly rougher."

"Do you think anyone would guess except you?"

"I am sure they would."

"I do not believe you!"

"I think it would be a mistake to put it to the test," the Marquis said drily.

There was a pause before she said:

"Now you have ruined everything! I was so confident that I would get away and remain undetected until I reached France."

"France?" the Marquis exclaimed. "Is that where you are going?"

She nodded.

"I have a friend in Paris. She is French, and I think if I could reach her she would hide me, and nobody would find me however hard they looked."

"And you really think you can travel from here to France by yourself? It is not only impossible but an extremely foolhardy idea!" the Marquis said.

Now that he had realised that he was talking to a girl and not a boy, he could see that she was undoubtedly attractive.

He thought he should have known sooner that the softness of her voice and its musical tones could never have belonged to anybody who was not feminine.

"Now you definitely have to help me," she said. "Will you find me a Courier to escort me to Paris? I can pay for his services."

"How much money have you?" the Marquis enquired.

"Twenty pounds in notes and coins," she replied, "and these . . ."

She put her hand into the pocket of her trousers and brought out two pieces which glittered in the moonlight.

The Marquis could see that one of them was a large crescent-shaped brooch set with diamonds, and the other was a collet of the same stones, which was undoubtedly worth a great deal of money.

"I can sell these," the girl said, "and live in comfort, I imagine, for quite a long time."

"And to whom would you sell them," the Marquis enquired, "even if you managed to cross the Channel in safety?"

She did not reply, but he knew she was attentive and listening as he went on:

"Any jeweller, seeing you dressed like that, would cheat you, and even if your friend will take you in and hide you, I imagine your parents will be searching for you and will find you sooner or later. Also, you will find that what money you have will not go very far in France."

"You are just making difficulties to scare me," the girl said accusingly.

"It would make things easier if you were frank with me," the Marquis said. "Start at the beginning. What is your name?"

"Cara."

"Is that all?"

"No, I have another name, but I do not intend to tell you what it is."

"Why not?"

"That is a leading question which I cannot answer."

"You must realise it is impossible for me to help you if you keep everything so secret."

"The only way I want you to help me is to get me to France. Surely that is not very much to ask?"

"It is a great deal," the Marquis replied. "First, you hide away in my carriage, in a place that I thought was inviolable from thieves. Secondly, you pretend to be a boy when you are a girl, and thirdly, you will not give me your name. What do you expect me to do, except perhaps hand you over to the Magistrates to deal with as they think best?"

The girl gave a little cry of horror. Then she said:

"You are frightening me! You know quite well you would not do such a thing."

"Do not be so sure."

"I am sure, even though you have a reputation for being heartless and ruthless."

The Marquis was startled.

"What do you mean by that?"

"Everybody talks about the Most Noble Marquis of Broome."

"Well, if they do, it is only fair that I should be able to talk about you. Give me your name."

"I refuse, utterly and completely refuse!"

"Why?"

"Because if I did, I know you would not help me."

The Marquis stared at her in surprise.

"I cannot imagine for a moment why you should say that. Actually I have helped a great number of people in trouble."

"That is not your reputation."

There was a pause before the Marquis said:

"I am not going to give you the satisfaction of being curious about me. I am trying to talk about you."

"Yes, I know, and as I have no wish to do so, it is far easier for us to discuss you. Other men are very jealous of you, but I expect you know that."

The Marquis laughed.

"I do not believe you are real," he said. "I must be dreaming this whole ridiculous situation. And incidentally, why are you wearing an Eton jacket?"

"It belongs to my cousin, who has outgrown it," Cara replied. "I smuggled it down from the attic and hid it in the back of the wardrobe until I was ready to run away."

"So you have been planning this for some time?"

"For over a week. I tried to think of another way of escaping, but this was the only way that seemed possible."

"You cut off your hair, dressed as a boy, then hid yourself in my chariot. How did you know it was mine?"

"I saw your coat-of-arms on the door, but actually I did not choose it because it belonged to you."

"Then what was the reason?"

"Because it was drawn by six horses, I knew it was going out of London tonight, which was what I wanted to do."

The explanation was so simple and reasonable that the Marquis smiled.

"So you would have taken any coach or carriage that looked as if it might be travelling a long distance?"

"Yes, but I am glad it was yours."

"Why?"

"Because whatever else they may say about you, you are a sportsman. That is why I know you will not turn me over to the Magistrates, and while you frighten me with talk of tramps robbing me and knocking me about, you will not abandon me."

The Marquis had to admit to himself that it was intelligent thinking, and he said after a moment:

"This is all very well, but I have to do something about you."

"I have told you what you can do."

"Are you prepared to give me the name of your friend in France?"

"No!"

"Why not?"

"Because you might later be forced into telling those who will undoubtedly pursue me where I have gone."

"Do you think I might be questioned?"

"I doubt it, but one never knows. There will be a hue and cry, and it would be much better if you were not involved too deeply."

"I think I am that already," the Marquis said. "And if there is a hue and cry, as you say, am I to pretend that I have never seen you, that you never travelled with me from London to the country?"

"How could you think of giving the enemy unnecessary information and encouragement?"

"They are your enemies, not mine."

Cara gave a little laugh.

"That is what you think!"

"What do you mean by that?" the Marquis asked.

"Nothing, but few men have as many enemies as you have. They are of course envious of your possessions and jealous of your personal successes, especially when it concerns lovely ladies."

The Marquis sat upright.

"How dare you talk like that!" he exclaimed. "I was obviously mistaken when I thought you were well bred."

Cara laughed again, and she was obviously not in the least abashed.

"What you are really saying is that you do not like the truth. If I was dressed in a ball-gown, simpering behind my fan, I would flatter you in the way you expect. But because I am pretending to be a boy I can say what I think."

"If I treated you like a boy, I would give you a good spanking!" the Marquis said grimly.

"I always understood that brute force was the last resort of idiots!" Cara retorted.

For a moment the Marquis glared at her. Then he leant back in his seat and chuckled.

"You are incorrigible!" he said. "Nobody has ever talked to me like this before."

"Then it is doubtless a salutary experience," Cara answered. "Although you will never see me again, perhaps you will remember what I have said to you and will be aware that there are those who will stab you in the back when you least expect it."

The Marquis laughed as if he could not help himself.

"If that happens, I shall doubtless remember what you have said too late."

"That will be your fault, now that I have warned you," Cara remarked.

Chapter Two

By the time the Marquis had ridden *Agamemnon* to the far end of the Park, both he and the horse were breathless.

By this time *Agamemnon* was beginning to acknowledge that he had met his master, and although he had tried every trick he knew to unseat him, the Marquis was still firmly in the saddle.

Both man and beast had developed a respect for each other during what had been a fiery and tempestuous battle from the moment they had left the stable-yard.

Now *Agamemnon* moved with a certain dignity, to show that he was still aware of his own consequence, but in the direction that the Marquis guided him.

He was thinking with satisfaction that he had a horse that was worthy of his own expertise, and that he would doubtless enjoy innumerable further battles with *Agamemnon*, but with the knowledge that they each had a wholesome respect for the other.

At the edge of the Park there was a flat piece of grassland on which the Marquis saw a number of his own horses galloping, ridden by stable-lads who were competing with one another.

He watched them for a few minutes, then rode towards his trainer, who held a watch in his hand.

The Marquis drew up beside him but did not speak until the man looked towards him and he was aware that he had finished his calculations.

"Well, Johnson?" the Marquis asked. "What is the verdict?"

Ted Johnson, who had been with the Marquis for six years and was acknowledged as one of the most experienced trainers in the country, smiled.

"*Fly-catcher*, M'Lord, will win the first big race in which Your Lordship enters him."

"You are sure of that?" the Marquis enquired.

"Very certain, M'Lord."

"And what about *Rollo*?"

"Given equal conditions, we shall certainly beat him," Ted Johnson replied with satisfaction.

The Marquis's eyes were on the horses trotting back to him now that they had finished their test-gallops.

They were all superbly bred. At the same time, there was one which any man with an eye for horses would know was outstanding, and that was *Fly-catcher*.

The Marquis had raced him in only one public race, then had withdrawn him into obscurity.

He knew without being told that he had what all owners dreamt of finding: a horse that was undefeatable in any race in which horses of the same age were running.

The previous year the Marquis had been confident of winning the Derby with a very fine horse which had been tipped to win quite early in the season.

Then, almost at the last moment, a rival had appeared on the scene in the shape of the Earl of Matlock's *Green Dragon*.

Naturally the Marquis, who if nothing else was a great sportsman, would have acceped his horse's defeat by *Green Dragon*, if he had not been suspicious of the way the Earl's horse had run.

His jockey had asserted that he had been "bumped

and bored" in a manner that was definitely against the rules.

But the Marquis had been aware that it was no use complaining to the Earl, whom he disliked and with whom he had had a number of skirmishes already over different Classic Races in which they both competed with a rivalry which had something very personal about it.

To put it in simple terms, the Marquis despised the Earl and the Earl detested the Marquis.

Although it was difficult to prove, the Marquis was quite certain that the Earl's instructions to his jockeys were to prevent his horses from winning, whatever methods they chose to use.

The Marquis, realising the brilliance of *Fly-catcher's* promise, had therefore taken him from his stables at Epsom and brought him and a number of his other horses down to Broome.

Keeping them out of sight of the racing fraternity, he had decided to produce *Fly-catcher* only at the last moment, as the Earl had done the previous year with *Green Dragon*.

There was no doubt that *Red Rollo* was an exceptional horse, but that was the only one belonging to the Earl that really constituted a threat to the Marquis's stable.

Because the Marquis had lain low, as it were, until now, *Red Rollo* was already being heavily backed, and when the time came the odds on him would shorten considerably.

"You are satisfied, Johnson?" the Marquis asked now. "He certainly looks in fine condition."

As he spoke he was watching *Fly-catcher* trot past him,

He knew by the grin on his rider's face that the horse had certainly come up to his expectations.

The other horses were being ridden by the stable-lads, but Bateson, who was a distinguished and well-known jockey, rode *Fly-catcher* up beside the Marquis.

"Good-morning, M'Lord!"

"Good-morning, Bateson," the Marquis replied. "What is your verdict?"

"Need Your Lordship ask?" Bateson answered. "*Fly-catcher's* the most outstanding horse I've ever had the privilege of riding!"

"I know that is high praise from you, Bateson."

"Keep him out of sight, M'Lord, or the first time anyone sees him he'll be an odds-on favourite."

The Marquis smiled.

He did not bother to say that he never betted on his own horses.

What he enjoyed was the satisfaction of being the winner. He disliked the type of owner who was concerned only with how much a horse could win him personally in hard cash.

Because he had no more to say, Bateson rode away, following the other horses who were returning to the stables.

The Marquis turned *Agamemnon*, and as he rode beside him Ted Johnson said:

"It'll give me great satisfaction, M'Lord, to beat His Lordship after the way he crowed over us last year."

The Marquis did not reply and Ted Johnson went on:

"I didn't know at the time, M'Lord, that Harwood, who were a-riding our horse, got two weals across his back when the Earl's jockey struck him."

The Marquis stared at his trainer before he asked:

"Do you mean to say that he was deliberately struck with a whip?"

"Yes, M'Lord," Johnson replied. "But Harwood's a quiet man and he'd no wish to make accusations against the Earl, which he said he'd find hard to substantiate in front of the Stewards."

"I have never heard anything so disgraceful!" the Marquis exclaimed. "If you had told me at the time . . ."

He stopped and said:

"No, Johnson, I think Harwood was right. It is always difficult to prove exactly what happens during a race, but you and I know that Harwood is a truthful man and would not lie about a thing like that."

"Exactly, M'Lord! And that's why he made no mention of it at the time. But he told me confidentially a little while ago that he'd no wish, even if Your Lordship asked him, to ride in this year's Derby."

"Why not?" the Marquis asked sharply.

"Because, M'Lord, there've been some unpleasant stories lately of jockeys who beat the Earl of Matlock having accidents on a dark night, and in one case being picked up in a ditch more dead than alive."

The Marquis stared at his trainer incredulously.

"Are you telling me the truth, Johnson?"

"It's what Harwood told me, M'Lord, and we both know that he's a Chapel-goer, known for being abstemious, and certainly no loose-mouthed talker."

"That is true," the Marquis conceded, "but I can hardly believe that the Earl of Matlock would sink to doing anything so utterly despicable and against all the rules of the Turf."

There was silence before Ted Johnson said:

"I've heard, M'Lord—but of course it's only the gossip of the race-course—that the Earl's in deep water and finding it hard to pay his debts."

The Marquis nodded his head as if it was no more than what he had expected.

Then, knowing it was a mistake to gossip for too long with one of his employees, he touched *Agamemnon* with his spur, which made the horse as restless as he had been before.

After a few bucks it was obvious that any further

conversation would be impossible, and the Marquis rode
him away.

He did not return to the house, but took *Agamemnon* over the gallop at a speed which satisfied them both.

He then rode for an hour over the fields to the west
of the Park before returning at a more leisurely pace
towards the house.

All the time he was riding the Marquis was thinking
of the Earl of Matlock, who he had known for some time
was an avowed enemy.

He was wondering how he could prevent him from
causing a scandal which would bode ill for the whole
racing world, which was something that the members of
the Jockey Club, like himself, tried to avoid by every
means in their power.

It was only as he was riding over the bridge which
spanned the lake that he remembered he had another
problem on his hands, and that was Cara.

The hard lines in which his lips had set while he was
thinking of the Earl relaxed a little as he remembered
her unexpected appearance in his carriage.

He recalled with some amusement the manner in
which she had refused to tell him of her identity and
various other details on their journey home.

She had sat opposite him, refusing to answer his
questions about herself and sparring with him in a
manner which he found original if extremely imperti-
nent, until she said:

"As I am very cold without an overcoat, I think, if
you do not mind, I will share your fur rug, and it would
be far more comfortable if I sat beside you."

She did not wait for him to agree, but getting up
and sitting down on the back seat beside the Marquis,
she pulled the sable rug which covered his knees over
her until it reached her chin.

As she did so, she gave a little shiver and said:

"Although I have no wish to impose upon you, I am
thinking that if you are to help me travel to France, I

shall have to borrow a cloak of some sort or I may die of cold on the journey."

"If you do, it will be your own fault!" the Marquis said unsympathetically. "You must have realised that this was the wrong time of year in which to travel."

"Of course I realised it," Cara answered, "but I would have braved the snows of the Himalayas or the ice of Antarctica rather than endure the fate that was awaiting me in London."

The Marquis looked towards her expectantly, thinking that perhaps she was going to tell him a little more about herself.

But she was sitting beside him in the shadows where the moonlight coming through the window did not reach, and he could only vaguely see the top of her head.

Cara gave a little chuckle.

"I know what you are expecting to learn," she said, "but you can just forget it. The only problem is whether you will be generous enough to send me to France with a Courier. Or, as I have already suggested, put me down in the nearest town to fend for myself."

"There is a much better alternative," the Marquis said, "and that is that you should return to where you come from. However unpleasant the conditions waiting for you there, you will encounter, I assure you, far worse in France, or even in some quiet market-town where the yokels will undoubtedly consider you a figure of fun."

"Do let us talk about something more interesting," Cara pleaded, "or perhaps you prefer not to talk while you are travelling."

"That is certainly an idea," the Marquis replied.

"Papa always said chattering females were intolerable, and never more so than when the movement of carriage-wheels loosened their tongues and they became indiscreet."

The Marquis smiled a little cynically, thinking that when he was alone with a woman it was not only her tongue that became loose, but that was something he could not say to Cara.

There was a little silence before she said:

"Now that I am beginning to feel warm, I also feel sleepy."

"Then I should go to sleep."

"I will," she answered, "if you promise not to take the opportunity of depositing me in a ditch, or returning me on a Stage-Coach to London."

"Do you really imagine I would do either of those things?" the Marquis asked.

He was aware from the movement of her body that she shook her head.

"No, you would consider that unsporting," she replied. "So I trust you to wake me first, whether it is when we reach Broome, or . . . when I have to . . . leave you. . . ."

Her voice trailed away on the last word and the Marquis was aware that she had fallen asleep.

A little while later her head slipped lower against the cushions in the corner of the carriage, and he lifted her legs up on the seat beside him.

He was aware that she was completely unconscious, lying curled up like a child in her cot.

He put out his hand and pulled the rug a little farther over her, then sat back and closed his eyes, thinking that he too would sleep.

Finding it impossible to do so, instead he puzzled as to who Cara could be and what in fact he was to do about her.

It was obvious that she was well bred and well educated, and he also had the idea that when he saw her in the daylight she would be attractive.

He knew that he would have to come to some conclusion about her before he reached Broome, for that he had brought from London a young woman dressed as a boy would be a piece of gossip that would sweep through the *Beau Monde* as if it were carried on the wind.

"I want no scandal!" the Marquis decided.

It was obvious that in that case the best thing he could do would be to agree to Cara's request that he set her down in a small market-town which they would pass through about half-an-hour before they reached the drive-gates of Broome.

Then he knew that such an action was impossible.

If Cara was unaware of the dangers she would encounter either as a young boy dressed as a gentleman, or worse still, as a girl dressed as a boy, the Marquis was not.

Because there was unrest over the whole country, which was something he had brought to the notice of the Cabinet again and again without much response, he was aware that in the towns where there was a great deal of hardship, it had naturally resulted in violent protests and a considerable amount of crime.

Three-quarters of the Cabinet were Peers of the Realm, and despite everything they heard and the Marquis's warnings, they were determined to repress the fomenting seeds of social revolution.

Freedom of speech had largely been lost during the Napoleonic Wars, and this suppression was still maintained.

Of the fifteen hundred men in the North of England who marched in protest at the price of bread, twenty-four had been condemned to death. Men were imprisoned, transported, or even hanged for protesting against low wages and their intolerable conditions of life.

The Marquis was convinced that there was a great deal more trouble ahead in the easily foreseeable future.

It was therefore impossible for him to think of leaving alone a young girl who had no idea of the conditions that existed both in Urban and in Rural England.

Her money, which she thought ensured her independence, would be taken from her as soon as she was noticed by any hungry labourer, and if she struggled, there was every likelihood of her losing her life, or being treated in a manner which did not bear thinking about.

"The best thing I can do," the Marquis decided, "is to send her to France as she wishes. Then she will no longer be my responsibility."

But the idea of washing his hands of a young woman who was undoubtedly a lady made him feel uncomfortable.

He had not decided exactly what he would do when he realised that his horses were already turning in at the lodge-gates of Broome and proceeding down the long drive of ancient oaks which led to the house.

Putting out his hand, he shook Cara by the shoulder to bring her back to wakefulness.

"What . . . is it? . . . What is the . . . matter?" she asked, sitting up straight.

"Wake up," the Marquis said. "We have arrived at my house, and I suppose, reluctantly, I must offer you a bed for the night."

Cara yawned, and the Marquis realised that she had been in a deep sleep when he had disturbed her.

"A . . . bed for the . . . night," she repeated, as if she found the words reassuring, then asked: "Tomorrow will you send me to France?"

"I will consider doing so," he replied, "but for the moment I would rather my servants did not see you in that extremely disreputable disguise."

As he spoke he slipped his fur-lined cloak from his shoulders, saying:

"You had better put this on, and for God's sake try to hide your trousers before I hand you over to my Housekeeper."

Cara chuckled.

"Do they shock you?"

"I am both surprised and shocked that a young woman of your age should be so immodest!"

"Rubbish!" Cara retorted. "If you are not shocked at the parties you give with your friends, and which are whispered about as being outrageous, you are certainly not shocked by me!"

The Marquis was about to ask her what she had heard about his parties when he realised that the horses had almost reached the front of the house and the servants were standing at the open door, from which a golden light poured over the stone steps.

"Cover yourself!" he ordered sharply.

He made it a command such as he might have given one of his troopers, but Cara merely chuckled.

At the same time, the Marquis was aware that he was pulling his extremely expensive fur-lined cape over her shoulders.

As he had already determined, she was very small.

By the time they reached the lighted Hall with its great carved gilt and ebony staircase, he was aware that she was completely covered by his cape, which reached almost to the ground and looked fairly respectable.

"I have an unexpected guest with me, Newman," he said to the Butler. "Ask Mrs. Peel to come to me as soon as possible."

"Very good, M'Lord," the Butler answered.

His impassive face expressed no surprise that the Housekeeper, who was nearly sixty, should be expected to get up and dress to accept His Lordship's instructions at two o'clock in the morning.

Without saying any more, the Marquis strode ahead into the Library, where he knew there would be sandwiches which were always ready for him on his arrival home.

Some hot soup would already be on its way up from the kitchen, where the Chef had been waiting, doubtless impatiently, for his arrival.

Only after the footman had offered the soup to Cara, which she had accepted, and the Marquis had taken a sip from a two-handled silver cup, did he say:

"Is there anything else you would like?"

It was the first time he had addressed Cara since they had entered the house, and he had in fact not even looked at her face, partly because he was afraid of what he might see.

Now as she sat beside the log fire which was burning brightly in the open grate, wrapped closely in his fur cape, he saw that she was different in appearance from what he had expected.

Because he was aware that she had fair hair, he had thought it would be complemented by blue eyes, and perhaps the "rose" look that was expected of a typical English maiden.

Instead, Cara had a heart-shaped face, and her eyes instead of being blue were decidedly green, slanting a little at the corners, which gave her a mischievous, provocative expression which the Marquis thought was somewhat in keeping with the manner in which she talked to him.

There were dimples on either side of her lips, which also curved upwards, and her face was balanced by a very small, straight, aristocratic nose.

As the Marquis inspected her with a penetrating look which those who were in awe of him said made them feel apprehensive and nervous, Cara's eyes twinkled, and her two dimples showed as she smiled before she asked:

"Am I worse or better than you thought I would be?"

"I am trying to make up my mind," the Marquis answered. "From your point of view it is definitely worse, because it would be impossible for me to send you to France looking as you do, even with a Courier."

"What do you mean by that?" Cara enquired.

"You are too young, you are too attractive, and you undoubtedly come from a respectable family," the Marquis answered.

"How can you be so ridiculous?" she asked. "You

know nothing about me. I am just a tiresome stranger who has intruded on your privacy because I was in need of a lift. I have no wish to be treated as if I were a Lady of Fashion—which I am not!"

"That, I think, is for me to judge," the Marquis replied, "and even if you are not a Lady of Fashion, you are certainly young and at an age when, whether you like it or not, you require a Chaperone."

Cara drank a little more of her soup before she said:

"What a bore you are! I shall now have to run away from you, as well as running away from . . ."

She stopped as if she realised that what she had been about to say would be too revealing.

Then as if she was aware that the Marquis was listening intently, hoping to catch her out, she said:

"As you are kind enough to give me a bed for the night, I would like to go to it now. I am so tired that I may otherwise be indiscreet, and that would be something I should very much regret in the morning."

"I will allow you to go to bed on one condition," the Marquis answered.

"What is that?"

"That you give me your sacred word of honour, that you swear on the Bible or anything else you consider holy, that you will not run away until you have discussed with me what would be the best thing for you to do."

There was silence for a moment. Then Cara said:

"Supposing I refuse?"

"Then regrettably," the Marquis said, "I shall either have to see that you are locked in for the night, or, which would be more uncomfortable as far as you are concerned, my Housekeeper will arrange for a maid to sleep in your room to make sure you do not escape."

Cara sat bolt upright, and there was no doubt that her eyes flashed at him as she said:

"How dare you suggest such a thing and make yourself responsible for me in a way I consider an imposition!"

The Marquis laughed.

"Now you sound more like a small tiger-cat than a young lady," he said. "Nevertheless, even a tiger-cat has to be put in a cage at night."

"Perhaps I made a mistake in choosing your carriage to convey me out of London," Cara said. "I did consider travelling with a young Buck who had only four horses, but as he had certainly had too much of the Prince Regent's wine to drink, I could doubtless have left him without his being aware of it."

The Marquis thought that she was too innocent to know that she might have found herself in a very unpleasant situation with a drunken Buck, but there was no point in his saying so, and he merely replied:

"My Housekeeper will be arriving at any moment. Do you wish to have one of the housemaids sleeping with you, or are you prepared to give me your word of honour?"

"How do you know I will keep it?" Cara enquired.

"In the same way that you know that I am a sportsman," the Marquis replied.

As he spoke the door opened, and as if the sound forced her to make up her mind, Cara said quickly:

"I give you my word of honour."

There was a faint smile on the Marquis's lips as he turned to greet his Housekeeper, who, bustling in black silk, looked quite unperturbed at being ordered from her bed at so late an hour.

* * *

The Marquis handed *Agamemnon* over to two grooms, who took the stallion's reins somewhat apprehensively.

He then walked up the steps, thinking that Cara might be as difficult to tame as the horse to whom he had just given a lesson which he would not forget.

In the Hall he handed his tall hat, gloves, and riding-whip to a footman, and Newman, the Butler, went ahead of him to open the door of the Breakfast-Room.

As he did so he said:

"I think the young lady has already begun breakfast, M'Lord. I told her you would not wish her to wait for Your Lordship's return."

The Marquis did not reply. He was aware that *Agamemnon* had made him nearly two hours late, but he had no intention of apologising to an unwanted and uninvited guest.

He only walked into the room, wondering as he did so what Cara would look like.

She was sitting at the round table in the window, and putting down her knife and fork she rose when he entered and dropped him a small curtsey.

She was dressed in a pretty but simple gown, which at first glance seemed to fit, but the Marquis's experienced eye realised a second or so later that it was too large round the waist and was therefore confined with a sash.

"As you have been riding, I wish you had let me come with you," she said reproachfully.

"Good-morning, Cara!" the Marquis said loftily, as if he reminded her of her manners. "If I had thought of it, which I did not, I would hardly have expected you to have in your pocket the requisite clothes for riding."

Cara gave a little chuckle as she sat down again at the table.

"I suppose you would not have considered letting me ride astride?"

"Most certainly not!"

The Marquis helped himself from the silver dish presented by one of the footmen while another poured out the coffee which he invariably drank on returning from riding, unlike his contemporaries who preferred brandy.

The Butler placed a rack of toasted bread in front of him, moved a silver dish containing a pat of golden

butter from his own Jersey cows a little nearer, and put a
bell at the Marquis's left hand.

Cara watched these attentions with an undoubted
twinkle in her eyes before she said:

"No wonder you do not get married! There is no
need when you have so many servants to cosset and fuss
over you. Mrs. Peel talks about you as if she were a
mother hen and you a wayward chick!"

The Marquis repressed a desire to laugh.

"If you are trying to provoke me, Cara," he said, "it
is too early in the morning. What is more, I am hungry."

"Only because you have been riding," Cara remarked. "I call it very inhospitable of you not to have let
me come with you. I am quite certain somewhere in this
house there is a riding-habit that I could wear."

"Why should you think that?" the Marquis enquired.

"Because, although I could hardly believe it, Mrs.
Peel has a whole wardrobe of clothes that have belonged
either to your relatives, alive or dead, or to guests who
have stayed here and left some of their garments
behind, and there are also suits that you yourself have
grown out of."

"Those you will kindly leave alone," the Marquis
said sharply.

"There are a great many of them," Cara replied,
"and they are far more suitable for me than the Eton suit
I was wearing. If I am going to France, I would travel
more comfortably dressed as a young man."

"If I find you wearing my clothes," the Marquis
said, "I promise you I will treat you as a man, and give
you a good hiding! It is what you deserve anyhow!"

"Now we are back to where we were last night,"
Cara said. "What are you going to do about me?"

"I have not decided," the Marquis replied, "but
before I do so, I want you to tell me a great deal more
about yourself than you have up to now."

There was silence until after a moment Cara asked:

"What exactly do you want to know?"

"First, who you are," the Marquis replied, "and secondly, why you have run away."

Cara pushed her plate to one side and put her elbows on the table, resting her chin on her hands.

Looking at her, the Marquis thought that with the light from the window on her hair, she looked exceedingly pretty, very young and different from any woman he had ever seen before.

He was used to conventional beauties, who, after being married for several years and having presented their husbands with several children including the much-needed heir, were prepared to enjoy themselves by flirting with the most attractive man they knew, who was invariably himself.

It was an unwritten law in the Social World that when a flirtation became an *affaire de coeur,* it should be kept as secret as possible, and husbands, even if they might suspect what was happening, had no wish to have their suspicions confirmed.

The Marquis of Broome, in his imperious, fastidious manner, had enjoyed the favours of some of the most lovely women in England, and there was no doubt that the Regent collected round him at Carlton House beauties whose attractions were unsurpassed by those of any other women in the world.

The Marquis could not quite determine why Cara's face had something irresistible about it that made him think it would be difficult, having once seen her, to forget what she looked like.

It might, he thought, be the effect of her short hair, which she had cut a little untidily and which was not arranged on her head.

Instead, it rioted in a manner which he was quite certain would seem irresponsible to any of the Dowagers who considered themselves to be leaders of the Social Scene.

At the same time, it had an attraction of its own

which he had noticed before only in Lady Caroline Lamb.

Whatever he felt about Cara, there was one thing that was obvious: she was a lady by birth, and as such he could not send her out alone, even with a Courier, on the long journey to France without behaving in what by his code was an irresponsible manner.

Without realising it, he had been staring at Cara, and now once again she interrupted his scrutiny to say:

"I hope you are taking in all my good points and not deliberately concentrating on my bad."

"I am not admiring you as a woman," the Marquis said sharply. "I am trying to decide what I should do about you as a person."

"Then as a person, or rather as an unwanted package which you have acquired by chance, send me to France!" Cara retorted. "I will go either as a boy or a girl, whichever you prefer, and having rid yourself of me, you need never think of me again."

The Marquis had a strange feeling that this might be difficult, and although it seemed incredible on such a short acquaintance, he had the uncomfortable feeling that he would worry about her.

"What I am going to suggest," he said, "is that you allow me to eat in peace. I will then decide, after you have told me your story, how and in what way I will help you. But I think I should warn you—I am very astute in knowing when somebody is lying to me."

Cara's laughter rang out, and it was a very spontaneous sound of delight.

"Really, you are so stupid," she said. "Do you suppose I do not know that? Of course no one could lie and you not be aware of it! You have an instinct, as I have, and my instinct tells me you will help me, however much you may prevaricate or try to wriggle out of the net in which I have caught you."

"Net?" the Marquis asked.

"Oh, do not be frightened," Cara said hastily. "If

you think I am trying to trap you into matrimony, you are very much mistaken. I have decided I will never get married, and that is final! And I do not intend to argue about it with anybody!"

She spoke so vehemently that the Marquis looked at her in surprise before he said:

"I presume, and now I am being intuitive, that the reason why you are running away is that you were to have been married."

Cara smiled at him.

"That is quick of you," she said, "and quite frankly, I am surprised that you are so perceptive."

"I find that remark almost an insult," the Marquis retorted.

"Not really," Cara answered. "Few men have any intuition at all. They just make up their minds what women are like, and they put them into a sort of pattern that has been evolved over the years, probably by their Nurses, their Governesses, their Tutors, and naturally by their mothers and fathers."

She gave a little laugh before she added:

"That means of course that to them a woman is a puppet, a doll, who has no feelings and certainly no intuition of her own."

"Is your suitor like that?" the Marquis asked. "And is that why you have no wish to marry him?"

He expected this to be too obvious a question for Cara to answer, but she gave a little shiver and said:

"He is horrible! Odious! Revolting! I would rather die than be his wife!"

"That might easily happen if I do not look after you," the Marquis said lightly. "But I do not suppose the gentleman in question is the only man in the world."

"He is the only man I am allowed to marry."

"And there is somebody else you would prefer?" the Marquis questioned.

She looked up at him.

"Now you are trying to embellish the story, to make

it seem more romantic. No! As I have already told you, I have no intention of marrying anybody, and that is why you are quite safe from me, if that is what is worrying you."

The Marquis threw back his head and laughed.

"You are certainly frank, my dear Cara, but not particularly complimentary!"

"Why should I be?" Cara enquired. "I have heard about your attractions and how women flutter round you like stupid moths round a flame, and I can assure you, if you went down on your knees and begged me to be your wife, I would say: 'No!' To be honest, I hate men—all men!"

Once again she was spitting out the words as she had last night when the Marquis had called her a "tiger-cat," and after a moment he asked quietly:

"What has a man done to you that you should speak like that?"

It was as though Cara drew in her breath, and there was an expression in her strange eyes he could not interpret. Then she said:

"I refuse to talk about the past. I am interested only in the future, and because you appear to have some sensibility, please try to understand that I must get away quickly, in case I am discovered here or anywhere else in England."

"And if you are?" the Marquis asked. "What will happen then?"

She looked at him, and he saw a fear in her eyes that he had never expected to see in any woman's before she said:

"You may think I am being theatrical or over-dramatic, but I will kill myself rather than accept what has been planned for me, which I can assure you is worse than any hell that was ever thought up by the Bible-thumpers."

Because although her words were dramatic she

spoke in a low, quiet voice, they rang in the Marquis's ears with a sincerity he could not ignore.

He did not laugh or argue with her.

He merely rang the bell, and when the Butler came hastily into the room he accepted another dish that was hot from the kitchen and waved away two others.

Without speaking, he had his cup replenished with coffee.

Only when the servants had once again left them alone was he aware that Cara was sitting back in her chair, looking at him appraisingly in the same manner in which he had looked at her.

He ate several mouthfuls of food before he asked:

"Well, what are your conclusions? Have you found my good points?"

Cara laughed.

"A few. I think you are authoritative, autocratic, and that you frighten most people, although you do not frighten me."

"Why not?" the Marquis asked.

"I will answer that question a little later, when I discover if I am right in what I am thinking about you now."

"I am disappointed," the Marquis said. "I thought after all you have said that you are so quick-witted that you make up your mind in a flash."

"I know I can trust you, if that is what you mean, and when you say you will help me, you will. But actually, I was considering you just now as a man."

"A species you tell me you dislike," the Marquis remarked.

"I loathe all men!" Cara replied. "But you have certain qualities that remind me of my father."

"As I hope that is a compliment, I would like to hear more," the Marquis said.

"Surprisingly, for it is certainly something I had not expected, I think you have a sense of humour."

"Thank you," the Marquis remarked somewhat mockingly.

"If you want to be flattered," Cara said, "there are plenty of women to do that, and from all I have heard, they include those not only of the *Beau Monde* but of an under-world which I am told no lady should know exists."

"Then why are you talking about it?" the Marquis asked.

"Because men like yourself find it attractive, and it interests me to learn why, when you have so much that is beautiful, fine, and perfect round you, you should also look at the gutters, or rather the Dance-Halls and the Houses of Pleasure, which no lady should mention."

"Then you should not be talking about them!" the Marquis said sharply.

"They interest me simply because it makes the world so much more complex and in a way more intriguing than the life that I am told I must enjoy as a débutante!"

She sighed before she went on:

"Which to my mind seems incredibly boring, and nothing more than a Marriage Market in which one sets out to catch a fish, and the bigger, the better!"

Again she was spitting out the words, and the Marquis laughed.

"Your metaphors are certainly very mixed," he said, "but I understand what you are saying. But surely no one can force you to marry someone you do not wish to marry?"

Cara stared at him before she said:

"Now that is the first really stupid remark you have made since we met!"

"Who is forcing you into marriage?" the Marquis asked. "Your father, or is it a Guardian?"

"You are being clever and trying to twist out of me what I do not intend to tell you," Cara answered. "If I tell you what you want to know, you will take me back a prisoner and hand me over to what I swear to you will be my certain death."

"I do not believe you!" the Marquis exclaimed. "What is more, I dislike hysterics at breakfast."

He spoke in a way which would have crushed most people he knew. Men or women, they would have either apologised or stammered into an embarrassed silence.

Cara merely laughed, and the sound seemed to ring round the Breakfast-Room and join with the wintry sunshine which was peeping through the grey clouds in the sky.

"You are very, very subtle," she said, "and I take back what I said about your being stupid. You are trying to make me lose my temper so that I will tell you what you want to know!"

She laughed again and went on:

"It is an old trick. In fact, it was thought out by the French Revolutionaries when they interrogated the aristocrats and forced many of them to incriminate themselves by their own words."

"How do you know that?" the Marquis asked with an amused smile.

"Curiously enough, unlike most girls of my age, I read!" Cara replied. "I will now whet your curiosity a little further: nothing I have read is half as bad, pernicious, or degrading as what I have encountered in real life."

She spoke in a way that made it difficult for the Marquis to say that he did not believe her or that she did not know what she was talking about.

She looked so young, yet, by again speaking in that quiet, controlled voice, she gave him the feeling that she was old and experienced.

He pushed his plate away and sat back in his chair.

"I wish you would trust me, Cara," he said. "If I am to help you as you want me to, you must be sensible enough to tell me the truth and let me judge whether it is as bad or as terrible as you believe it to be."

As he spoke he looked directly at Cara and met her eyes.

For a moment it seemed as if they were linked together by something magnetic, yet invisible, something which joined them in a way which made it difficult for her to look away from him.

Then as she told herself that she must not listen to him, and that once again he was trying to trap her and find out what she had no intention of saying, the door of the Breakfast-Room opened.

"The Earl of Matlock, M'Lord!" the Butler announced.

For a moment the Marquis felt he could not have heard correctly what the servant had said.

But into the room came the man he most disliked, followed by two others.

There was silence.

Then Cara gave a little scream like that of a small animal caught in a trap.

"Uncle . . . Lionel!" she exclaimed, and her voice vibrated with fear.

Chapter Three

For a moment the Marquis could only stare at the Earl in astonishment.

He was a middle-aged man and had been considered good-looking when he was young, but his eyes were too close together.

He now not only looked debauched, but the enmity and hatred with which he regarded the Marquis had etched lines on his face that were unmistakable.

As he entered the room he was smiling unpleasantly and there was a light of triumph in his expression which the Marquis at first found hard to understand.

Deliberately he did not rise to his feet but asked:

"May I enquire why you are here, Matlock, so early in the morning?"

As he spoke he realised that the Earl was in riding-clothes, his boots were covered with dust, and he was holding in his hand a thin riding-whip.

It was obvious that he had ridden hard and fast, and a glance at the two men with whom he had come told the Marquis the same story.

One was a sharp-faced, long-nosed, sandy-haired individual, not unlike a ferret; the other, to his surprise, was wearing the white bands of a Cleric beneath his riding-coat.

He had grey hair and a thin, cadaverous face which gave the impression that he was half-starved.

Ignoring Cara, the Earl walked across the room to the breakfast-table to confront the Marquis.

"I am here, Broome," he said, "to inform you that at last I have you where I have always wanted you—at my mercy!"

The Marquis's expression did not alter, but there was a wary look in his eyes as he replied:

"I have not the slightest conception of what you are talking about, and I think, Matlock, you should explain not only yourself but also the presence in my house of two other people I have not invited."

"Let me introduce them," the Earl said with a grandiose gesture. "My Solicitor, Israel Jacobs of Lincoln's Inn, and the Reverend Adolphus Jenkins, whom you are unlikely to have met, as his clients are mostly from the Fleet Prison."

He spoke mockingly. At the same time, there was an undeniable note of spite in his voice, which echoed the elation he was feeling.

His two companions stood just inside the door, and the Marquis was aware that Cara had retreated from the table until she stood against the panelled wall as far from the Earl as it was possible to get.

The Marquis also had the idea that she was longing to bolt from the room, which was impossible owing to the fact that the Earl's companions were standing by the door, and the windows which opened onto the garden were tightly closed.

"I am still at a loss to understand why you are here," the Marquis said after a moment's ominous silence.

"Let me put it to you more plainly," the Earl replied. "I am accusing you, Broome, of abducting and doubtless of ravishing a minor."

The Marquis stiffened but did not move, and the expression on his face did not change, while Cara gave another shrill cry.

"That is a lie! He did not abduct me. I hid myself in his carriage."

The Earl did not turn his head as she spoke, and indeed he gave no indication that he had even heard what she said.

His eyes were on the Marquis as he said slowly and distinctly:

"I am prepared, Broome, to give you a choice between standing trial for a crime which entails transportation, or marrying my niece and giving me ten thousand pounds for the privilege."

As he finished speaking there was a silence that seemed to the Marquis to be more eloquent than any words.

He saw only too clearly that the Earl held a trump-card in his hand and would not hesitate to play it.

He was well aware that not only had the successes of his horses over the Earl's enraged and embittered him as a rival, but he had on numerous occasions found it necessary to report to the Jockey Club infringements of the laws of racing which involved the Earl's jockeys and the Earl's horses.

On one occasion a horse had actually been disqualified after the Earl had ostensibly won the race, and the prize had gone to the Marquis's, which had come in second.

He had known then that the Earl would never forgive him, and now it flashed through his mind that he had inadvertently put himself at the mercy of a man who was an avowed enemy and was overjoyed at the chance to take his revenge.

What was so galling was that the Marquis had for years escaped every bait offered to him and every trap set for him as the most eligible bachelor in the *Beau Monde*.

There was no aristocratic family in the length and breadth of England which would not welcome him as a son-in-law.

But he had long ago decided that he had no wish to be married and no intention of being caught by the ambitious parents who thronged the Mayfair Ball-Rooms.

This decision, once it was known, had evoked a great deal of gossip and had even been lampooned by the satirical pens of the cartoonists.

Vaguely he had thought that at some time he must beget an heir, and he knew exactly the type of wife who would fulfil his requirements as the Marchioness of Broome.

This certainly did not involve espousing himself to some unfledged, ignorant girl with whom he knew he would become bored stiff within a few weeks of the Wedding Ceremony.

There was plenty of time for him to pick and choose and, with his fastidious, critical taste, to take a wife who would fit into the pattern of his life and do exactly what he required of her.

That he should be confronted with an ultimatum such as the Earl had brought him now was something that had never occurred to him even in his wildest nightmares.

Quickly and intelligently he sought a way out.

In his usual calm, rather dry manner, he said:

"I can scarcely believe that what you are saying, Matlock, is not some poor joke in very bad taste."

"It is no joke, I assure you," the Earl replied sharply. "Mr. Jacobs is prepared, if you refuse, to take my petition, which I have already signed, to the Chief Constable of the County. You can then expect to be arrested within a few hours and taken to the Old Bailey to await trial."

He paused to see the effect of his words before he continued:

"On the other hand, the Reverend Mr. Jenkins has in his possession a Special Licence which I obtained before I left London, which will enable him to marry you to my niece in your private Chapel. The choice is yours!"

The Marquis drew in his breath.

He was just about to say that he would see the Earl and his underlings damned first, when Cara gave another scream and walked into the centre of the room.

"If you think I will marry the Marquis in such circumstances," she said furiously, "then you are very much mistaken! I ran away because you tried to marry me to that filthy, beastly man, and I have made up my mind that I will not marry anybody ever, and you cannot make me!"

The Earl turned to look at her for the first time since he had come into the room, and as the Marquis watched him there was no doubt of the hatred he could see in his eyes.

"Are you again defying me?" he demanded. "Well, I am prepared to concede that you have chosen for yourself a more impressive lover than Forstrath, but you will marry him and I will have no hysterics!"

"I am not hysterical!" Cara replied fiercely. "I am only telling you that I will not marry the Marquis or that beast Sir Mortimer Forstrath, and no Marriage Service is legal if the bride says: 'No'!"

Her eyes were blazing as she spoke, and her words seemed almost to tumble over one another.

Without replying, the Earl raised his hand and struck her so violently on the side of her face that she fell to the ground.

Then, so quickly that the Marquis could hardly believe it was happening, the Earl transferred the thin whip he had been holding in his left hand to his right, and brought it down with all his strength on Cara's body as she lay on the floor at his feet.

He hit her twice before the Marquis jumped to his feet, shouting:

"Stop! How dare you strike a woman in my house!"

He pushed the breakfast-table in front of him to one side and was advancing towards the Earl with his fists clenched menacingly when Israel Jacobs moved from the doorway to confront him.

To the Marquis's astonishment, he held a pistol in his hand.

"Stay where you are, M'Lord," Israel Jacobs ordered. "A Guardian has his rights and is within the law if he punishes his Ward as he sees fit."

As his Solicitor spoke, the Earl glanced over his shoulder before he struck Cara again.

"That is right," he said, "and by the time I have finished with this tiresome little renegade, she will marry the Devil himself, if I tell her to!"

He raised his whip again, and as it struck her back Cara gave a shriek of pain.

The Marquis calculated that by moving quickly he might be able to knock the Solicitor's pistol from his hand, and the chances of success without having a bullet blown through him were about fifty-fifty.

Then as he flexed his muscles he became aware that the Parson also was pointing a pistol at him, and while it was held in a shaky and certainly unprofessional hand, it was still an unmistakably lethal weapon.

With two muzzles pointed at his heart, the Marquis knew he had not even an odds-against chance of escaping injury, if not death.

As he stood irresolute, Cara screamed again, and feeling as if he signed his own Death Warrant the Marquis said:

"Very well, Matlock. You win this skirmish, which I concede is a well-thought-out piece of criminal blackmail."

The Earl lowered his arm.

"I am glad you appreciate it, Broome. And now perhaps we can get down to business."

The Marquis, with tremendous self-control, did not reply.

He only walked across the room to stand in front of

the fireplace, wondering desperately as he did so if there was any possible escape and, if so, what it could be.

The Solicitor and the Parson lowered their weapons but did not replace them in their pockets, and as the Earl looked down at Cara, the Marquis had an undeniable impression that he just barely restrained himself from kicking her.

"It is a pity," the Earl said to her, "that your future husband has, by surrendering so quickly, prevented me from giving you the thrashing you so richly deserve! How dare you run away from my house!"

He waited as if he expected her to reply, then went on:

"But who knows? I may be able to turn your position in the Social World to a better advantage than I would have gained by your marriage to Mortimer Forstrath."

As he spoke in a sneering, unpleasant manner that seemed almost to poison the atmosphere, the Marquis was suddenly aware of whom he was speaking.

He was not acquainted with Sir Mortimer Forstrath, who was a man he would never have acknowledged as a friend, knowing that he was greatly disliked in the Clubs of which he was a member.

He could not recall at the moment the specific reason for this attitude, but he could well believe that Forstrath was not a suitable husband for Cara.

As the Earl finished speaking he walked towards the Marquis and stood a few feet from him, and the two men glared at each other like pugilists in a ring.

Then the Earl said in the same unpleasant, sneering tone of voice and with a smile on his thin lips:

"I shall require your cheque first, Broome. The ceremony can take place immediately afterwards."

As he was speaking, Cara dragged herself from the floor up onto her feet.

She was very pale, except for one cheek which was

red from the impact of her uncle's hand when he had struck her down.

The weals across her back were agonising, but her only thought was that if she could leave the room she would somehow get to the stables and, taking a horse, gallop away before anyone could stop her.

It flashed through her mind that the money and jewellery she had brought with her were upstairs, but at the moment that was immaterial.

What was important was that she should escape before she was forced to marry the Marquis, for she knew that her uncle was not speaking lightly.

When she had run away last night from his house in Grosvenor Square, she had known that nothing she could say, no pleading or begging for mercy, would prevent him from marrying her to Sir Mortimer Forstrath.

He wanted the money, he wanted to be rid of her, and he had already threatened to beat her unconscious if she argued with him any further.

It had never entered her head that in imposing herself on the Marquis, her uncle would not only find her but would use the situation as a means of providing himself with the money he so desperately needed, and at the same time of having his revenge on his greatest enemy.

Slowly, step by step, hoping that nobody was noticing her, she crept towards the door.

But just as she reached it, Israel Jacobs moved several steps backwards to stand in her way.

There was no need for him to speak, he just stood there, and with a little sigh Cara realised that she was defeated.

From the other side of the room the Marquis said:

"Let us talk this over sensibly, Matlock. I will give you the money, but as you are well aware, I did not abduct your niece, and there is no reason for me to marry her. She was well chaperoned last night by my Housekeeper, a very respectable woman."

"No Magistrate, Jury, or Judge would consider a paid servant a sufficient Chaperone for a young innocent girl who has spent a night with the noble Marquis of Broome!" the Earl sneered.

As if he wished to provoke the Marquis even further, he added:

"You have had your fun, Broome, and now you must be a sportsman and pay for it!"

Only by exerting the greatest control did the Marquis prevent himself from knocking the Earl down.

"I will make it fifteen thousand pounds," he said quietly.

The Earl laughed.

"You are a very rich man, Broome, and it will be a considerable advantage for me to be able to claim a close relationship with you. I shall hope to enjoy a great deal more than money in the years ahead."

What the Earl was saying was irrefutably true, and the Marquis knew that he would make the very most of a family connection between them. It was infuriating that he should also demand an astronomical sum in recompense.

As if he felt he had driven the Marquis too far, the Earl said briskly:

"Suppose we get on with the business on which I have come? As I imagine you do not keep your cheque-books in the Breakfast-Room, I propose we should repair to your Study, if that is where they are."

That the Earl was taking command and ordering him about in his own house was in itself an insult which was hard to stomach, but the Marquis merely walked across the room and opened the door.

Cara was standing by it, and he glanced at her perfunctorily, and waited, obviously expecting her to precede him.

Moving slowly, as if in pain, she walked ahead, the

Marquis followed, and behind him, delighted by the success of his campaign, came the Earl and his two attendants.

Because she did not know the way, Cara waited until the Marquis was beside her; then, knowing that there was nothing she could do, she let him lead her to the Study door, which was opened hastily by a footman.

They entered the large, comfortable room where the walls were hung with paintings by Stubbs, the chairs were covered with leather, and there was a flat-topped desk furnished with a huge gold ink-pot and a blotter on which was the Broome coat-of-arms.

As the Marquis walked towards his carved, high-backed writing-chair, Cara wondered once again if there might be a chance of escaping.

But with her uncle and his two henchmen behind her she knew it was impossible, and because she felt her legs could no longer hold her, she sat down on the hearth-rug.

Turning her back to the room, she held out her hands towards the big log-fire.

As she did so she was unaware that the blood from the weals on her back caused by her uncle's whip had begun to seep through the thin gown she was wearing.

The Marquis looked up from his desk and saw them, and his lips tightened into a harder line than they were already as he opened the drawer in front of him.

As he started to write the cheque, the Earl saw that in the corner of the Study was a table containing a grog-tray on which were various decanters.

Without asking permission, he walked across to it and poured for himself and the two men with him a large amount of brandy.

They took the glasses from him eagerly. Then he raised his own in the direction of the Marquis to say:

"I am of course prepared to drink, My Lord, to your happiness."

The Marquis did not even look up, and the Earl continued mockingly:

"You will find Cara hard to handle and extremely headstrong. So I think it appropriate that my wedding-present to you should be the whip I use to make her obey me. You will certainly need it yourself in the future!"

As he spoke he walked towards the desk and flung down in front of the Marquis the whip he had still been carrying in his hand.

The Marquis ignored both the act and the Earl's remark. He merely signed the cheque, then rose to his feet, leaving it on the table.

The Earl reached out and appeared almost to snatch it in his desire to make it his.

Then he looked at it carefully as if to see that he had not been tricked, and said:

"That is satisfactory. Now perhaps, Broome, you will show us the way to your Chapel, which I presume you as a God-fearing man keep in use?"

Again he was sneering, but the Marquis merely looked towards Cara, who at her uncle's words had turned her face from the fire.

Realising that they were all waiting for her, she slowly rose to her feet.

She was even paler than she had been when they had left the Breakfast-Room, except for the imprint of the Earl's hand, which was like a red flag on her cheek.

She walked past her uncle with her chin held high, and only as the Marquis opened the door for her and she started to walk through it did an idea flash into her mind.

As she stepped outside into the passage, she turned suddenly, slammed the door to, and turned the key in the lock.

Then, lifting her skirts, she was running as swiftly as she could towards the Hall and out through the front door.

As she had anticipated, the three horses which had

brought her uncle and the two men with him to Broome were outside, each held by a groom.

Cara sped down the steps and literally flung herself into the saddle of the first horse she came to.

She made no pretence of riding side-saddle but sat astride, and picking up the reins set off before the grooms could grasp what was happening.

As they stared after her she rode the horse away from the house and towards the bridge which spanned the lake.

She had not gone far before she realised that the horse she was riding was tired after what had been a long and doubtless exhausting journey from London.

She guessed that it had been quicker for her uncle to ride across country than to take the road.

Because he must have been afraid that she might leave Broome before he had arrived, he had travelled at a speed which had exhausted the horse under him.

Cara had no whip and no spurs, and although she dug her heels into the horse's sides, she found before she had reached the end of the drive that the animal would go no faster than a trot.

She glanced over her shoulder, and as she reached the lodge-gates she could see in the distance that there were two horses following her.

It was not difficult to guess that her uncle had forced the Marquis to ring the bell, or had done so himself, and a servant had answered the summons to unlock the sliding door.

Outside the lodge-gates was a road running both right and left, and because she remembered that the way to London was to the right, Cara turned to the left.

It was nothing more than a small lane which twisted along the side of the high brick wall which at this point bordered the Marquis's Estate.

She rode on, doing everything in her power to hurry her mount, but knowing that she was having little effect

Then, because she was afraid of the two men following her, when she saw an open gate which led to a field in the centre of which was a small copse, she rode towards it.

She hoped that she might hide there, but even as she reached the first trees she looked back and saw a rider coming down the lane she had just left, and she knew with a constriction of her heart that it was her uncle.

She realised then that the two riders who pursued her must have divided at the lodge-gates and her uncle had turned to the left.

He was beating the horse on which he was riding so that it moved at a far greater speed than anything she had been able to produce from her horse.

As the hedges were low and leafless at this time of the year, Cara was aware even as she was about to enter the wood that her uncle had seen her.

Because she now realised that her effort to escape was hopeless, she thought it more dignified to turn and ride back towards him.

He was red in the face from his exertions, and as he met her in the middle of the field, he shouted furiously:

"Damn and blast you! What the hell do you think you are doing?"

"Trying to escape from you, Uncle Lionel!" Cara replied with a flash of spirit, which was echoed by a feeling of despair at her fruitless effort to get away.

"You will come back with me!" the Earl said. "If the Marquis has run away in the meantime, I will beat you until you wish you had never been born."

"I have wished that often enough since I have been with you!" Cara retorted.

Her uncle turned his horse back towards the gate through which they had entered the field, and because there was nothing else she could do, Cara followed him.

When they reached the road and were riding side by side, the Earl said:

"If you were not so pig-headed you would realise I am doing you a good turn in marrying you to Broome. Your social position will equal that of any other woman in the land who is not Royal."

"I shall also be married to a man who will loathe and despise me because I am your niece!"

Instead of being angry, the Earl chuckled.

"At last I have beaten him!" he said with a tone of satisfaction.

Cara did not speak, and he went on:

"He has sneered at me, condescended to me, and has been a thorn in my flesh for the last five years! Now I am the winner, and 'Mr. High and Mighty' has to eat the dust!"

"You have the money you wanted," Cara said. "Let me go, Uncle Lionel. Say you could not find me and have no idea where I have gone. I will disappear and you will never see me again."

"I am not going to argue with you," the Earl replied. "You will marry Broome, and thank God, if there is one, on your knees! No Guardian could do more for a niece who has been nothing but a headache since he has known her."

"You are not doing it to please me," Cara said. "You always hated Papa because you were jealous of him, and that is why you hate me. The only reason I shall thank God is because I shall no longer have to live with you!"

The Earl chuckled and it was an unpleasant sound.

"So you have still got some spirit in you, have you?" he asked. "I hoped I had beaten it out of you. It is a pity you are not marrying Mortimer Forstrath, for he would have had no nonsense with you."

Cara did not answer.

She merely saw the house lying ahead of them and knew that her uncle was right in that whatever her life with the Marquis might be, it would be infinitely preferable to what she would have suffered as the wife of Sir Mortimer Forstrath.

She suddenly felt limp and faint, not only from losing the battle against her uncle but also because of the weals on her back, which were hurting intolerably.

She rode ahead so that she need not listen to the Earl's sneers and jeers, and because she was afraid that she might collapse, she tried to think only of keeping in the saddle until she reached the house.

Somehow, she managed it.

As a groom went to the horses' heads, she swung her leg over the saddle and slid to the ground.

Only as she reached it and knew that she must somehow walk up the steps did she feel a darkness coming up from the earth beneath her feet to swallow her up.

* * *

Cara came back to consciousness to find herself sitting in a carved wooden pew in the Marquis's private Chapel.

Somebody was holding a handkerchief dipped in *eau de Cologne* against her forehead, and another hand held a glass of brandy against her lips.

She tried to push it away, then she heard the Marquis say in his dry, impersonal voice:

"Drink it. You will feel better."

Because it was easier to obey than to argue, Cara took a sip and felt the fiery liquid seep down her throat and into her body.

It took away a little of the darkness that was still hovering round her, and she knew from the way the Marquis moved the glass against her lips that he wished her to drink again.

She did so, and now the last remnants of the darkness cleared and she realised where she was and what had happened.

"She will be all right now," a voice said.

The handkerchief was moved from her forehead,

and as she looked up she saw that the Marquis was standing beside her.

It was difficult to read the expression in his eyes, but she knew by the tightness of his lips and the squareness of his chin that he was very angry, although she thought it was not with her.

"Would you like a little more?" he asked, and although his voice was impersonal, she had the feeling that he was in fact somewhat compassionate.

She shook her head.

"No-no . . . thank . . . you."

"In which case, let us get on with the ceremony!" her uncle said sharply.

Cara turned her head.

She saw that he was leaning against another pew and that the Parson he had brought with him was standing at the altar-steps, holding a Prayer-Book in his hand.

In his dusty riding-boots and with the only sign of his Holy office being the two white bands at his neck, he looked shockingly incongruous.

But Cara was quite certain that her uncle would have seen to it that he was properly ordained and that the Marriage Service said by him and the Special Licence would be entirely legal and binding.

She knew in that moment that she had failed and there was no escape, although any marriage in such circumstances was a farce and an outrage against a Sacrament of the Church. But there was nothing she could do about it.

The Marquis was not looking at her but had walked a few paces away to wait for her to come stand beside him.

Almost instinctively and without conscious thought she glanced towards the back of the Chapel and saw that in the doorway, either to prevent her from leaving or to prevent people from entering, Israel Jacobs was standing.

His eyes were on her and she felt as if he too mocked at her helplessness.

Her uncle crossed to her side.

He put out his hand, and because she could not bear to touch him, she held on to the pew in front of her and pulled herself to her feet.

As she did so, she knew that the scars on her back were stiffening, and it was with difficulty that she prevented herself from giving a murmur of pain.

Then, because she would not be treated with derision, and if nothing else she still had her pride, she put up her hand, even though it was painful, to pat her untidy curls into place.

Then, without even glancing at her uncle, she walked the short distance up the aisle to stand beside the Marquis.

He did not look at her as the Parson began the Service, reading slowly and at times inaudibly from the Prayer-Book he held in his hands.

"I, Ivo Alexander Maximilian, take thee, Cara Matilda, to my wedded wife."

Cara heard the Marquis repeating the words calmly and quite expressionlessly, and she felt she must be dreaming.

Then, as if it were a dream, she heard her own voice:

"I, Cara Matilda, take thee, Ivo . . ."

Even as she spoke, she knew that she had lost not only her freedom but also her dreams.

Although she had sworn never to marry, somewhere far away at the back of her mind she had believed that one day she would find a man who was different from all the others she had known.

But that had seemed impossible when she was hating first her uncle, then the monster he had produced as her future husband.

Then, with a terror that had seemed to sweep through her body like forked lightning, she had believed that all men were fiends, or rather wild animals who pursued her and from whom she had to escape.

Her uncle's cruelty, the hatred she felt for him, and the horror that she had known when she had met Sir Mortimer had combined to make her determined that never, never would she be owned by a man!

She would remain free, unless by some miracle, which seemed very unlikely, she found a man whom she could trust because she loved him.

Now, when she least expected it, when she thought she had run away to become independent, she had been captured and was to be chained to the Marquis for the rest of her life.

"Those whom God hath joined together let no man put asunder!"

As the Parson spoke the words it seemed to Cara that it was the voice of doom.

She knew that somehow, in some way she could not for the moment envisage, she had to escape from the Marquis.

Chapter Four

The Marquis stood at the door watching the Earl and his two companions ride away under the oak trees.

Only long years of exerting control over his feelings prevented him at the last moment from striking the Earl and wiping the smile of satisfaction and derision from his face.

When they left the Chapel, the Earl had said in the same sneering voice he had used before:

"I presume, Broome, you are not hospitable enough to offer us a glass of champagne to drink on this auspicious occasion?"

The Marquis had not replied. He had walked away from Cara's side the moment they were married and strode ahead along the passage which led from the Chapel back to the Hall.

When they reached it, he did not speak but merely stood looking at the Earl in a manner which told him in no uncertain terms that he was to leave his house.

He knew by the expression on the Earl's face that he was trying to decide whether to provoke him further, or whether it would be wiser to leave him in silence.

Finally he chose the latter, and walked through the front door and down the steps to mount his tired horse in a manner which was a flourish of defiance, if nothing else.

The Solicitor and the Parson followed him, and they rode away with the Marquis watching them with such hatred vibrating from him as would have intimidated any ordinary man.

Then with a last glance at the three riders vanishing into the distance, the Marquis called to one of the grooms who had been holding their horses and were now preparing to make their way back to the stables.

"Ben!"

"Yes, M'Lord?"

"Saddle *Thunderer* and bring him to me immediately!"

"Very good, M'Lord."

The Marquis, feeling that he could not face Cara, did not go back into the house.

Instead, he walked from the front door across the gravel sweep in front of it and down over the lawn towards the lake.

When he reached it, the thin cover of ice that had been there first thing in the morning had broken, and now the ducks and swans were swimming on the water in the centre of it.

A pale sun was seeping through the dark clouds to throw a golden light on them.

The Marquis did not see it. Instead, he saw and felt only the humiliation he had just endured at the hands of an enemy.

It was, he thought, the first time he had been defeated in a battle in which he had never had a chance of being the victor.

It had all happened so quickly that he could hardly believe that what had occurred was not just a figment of his imagination.

And yet it was an undeniable fact that he was now married, and to a woman he had seen for the first time only last night in strange and not particularly admirable circumstances.

"Married!"

The word seemed to echo round him, and for the moment his brain could not be stimulated into telling him how he could cope with a situation he had never envisaged, and which was completely incompatible with everything that he had planned for himself now and in the future.

He stood staring at the lake until he heard the sound of a horse's hoofs behind him and the clinking of harness, and turned to see one of his finest stallions approaching.

The horse was fresh, and the Marquis knew that only by taking violent exercise could he somehow assuage the tumult that seemed to be flooding over him like a tempest.

He flung himself into the saddle, and without a word to the groom he galloped away, taking a route through the Park to where he knew he would be able to ride *Thunderer* until they were both exhausted.

* * *

In the house, Cara, having seen her uncle depart, walked towards the staircase and climbed it slowly, feeling that every step was an effort as the pain in her back increased.

For the moment, because she was concerned with the physical agony she was enduring, she could not think clearly of her marriage to the Marquis or what it entailed.

All she wanted was to lie down and be alone.

Only when she reached her bedroom did she know that after the beating her uncle had given her and her collapse when she returned to the house after trying to escape, she was too exhausted to care.

Wearily she struggled towards the bed, and lying down on it slowly so as not to hurt her back, she closed her eyes and hoped that she might become unconscious. . . .

* * *

Hours later Cara awoke from a sleep that had been half a faint to begin with; then, because she had no wish to face reality, she had gone into what was a self-induced coma.

She tried to turn and found that the blood from the wounds on her back had dried onto the pillow on which she was lying, and she gave a little cry of pain, which brought somebody to her bedside.

It was Mrs. Peel, the Housekeeper, and Cara found it hard to remember who she was.

"Are you awake, M'Lady?"

"I . . . suppose . . . so."

"I wonder if Your Ladyship feels strong enough to move to another room? Everything's prepared for you, and I think, Your Ladyship, I should put some salve on your back, then you can get into bed properly and rest."

Because it was easier to agree than to argue, Cara let Mrs. Peel lead her from the room she occupied and down the corridor to the South Wing of the house.

She was too tired to be interested, and it was only later that she realised she had been put in a bedroom that had always been occupied by the mistresses of Broome and had last been used by the Marquis's mother.

But when she first entered it she was aware only of pain and exhaustion, and like some small animal that had been hurt she wanted to crawl into a hole out of reach of everything that was frightening.

It was very painful when her gown was being removed, but the salve was some comfort as Mrs. Peel applied it to the broken skin, then covered it with a soft lint.

She was given something warm to drink, which she thought was honey and milk, but she was not curious enough to enquire.

Then, half-lifted by Mrs. Peel, she found herself in

the large bed with massive posts carved and gilded which supported a canopy of cupids rioting amongst leaves and flowers.

But this had no reality for Cara, who could think only of putting her head down on the pillow and shutting her eyes.

The curtains were drawn over the three long windows, and left alone she tried to close her brain against thought and concentrate only on trying to sleep.

*   *   *

The Marquis did not return to the house until late in the afternoon.

As he walked in through the front door, the Butler, taking the Marquis's tall hat, gloves, and riding-whip, thought he looked drawn and considerably older than he had that morning.

The servants were naturally agog at what had happened, being well aware that their master had been in the Chapel with a Parson and the strange young lady who had arrived unexpectedly the night before.

Although Mrs. Peel was the soul of discretion, the housemaids could not resist relating below-stairs that the young lady who had arrived had short hair and wore an Eton suit under His Lordship's fur-lined cloak.

Speculation as to who she could be and why she had come to Broome in such a strange manner had been the sole topic of conversation from the knife-boy to the eldest housemaid.

"There's a gentleman arrived from London to see Your Lordship," the Butler said respectfully to the Marquis. "I've shown him into the Study, M'Lord."

"From London?" the Marquis queried.

For a moment he thought it might be Henry Hansketh, then knew it was too soon to expect him.

His first impulse was to say that he wished to see nobody, but convention and good manners told him that was something he could not do when somebody had journeyed all the way from London.

Accordingly, knowing that what he wanted was a bath and something to eat, he walked towards the Study, hoping his unexpected caller would not keep him long.

A footman opened the door, and as he entered the room he saw to his surprise that the gentleman, who apparently had not given the Butler his name, was a member of the Royal Household.

"Good-afternoon, Bingham," the Marquis said. "I must apologise if I have kept you waiting. I was not expecting you to visit me."

"I thought it right to bring you the information myself," Mr. Bingham replied, "that His Majesty expired at thirty-two minutes past eight o'clock last night."

"The King is dead!" the Marquis exclaimed.

It came actually as a surprise, even though it was something that had been expected for so long.

Like the Regent, the Marquis and many other Courtiers had begun to think that the King would never die.

"He is dead," Mr. Bingham replied, "and as today is the anniversary of the execution of Charles I, the Proclamation of the new King's accession will not be made until Monday."

"And of course he expects me to be present," the Marquis said almost as if he spoke to himself.

"That is why I came here with all speed, My Lord. His Majesty is already asking for you."

"Thank you, Mr. Bingham," the Marquis said. "And now let me offer you a glass of wine, or would you prefer brandy?"

"Wine, if you please, My Lord."

"You will of course stay the night," the Marquis went on, "and we will leave for London first thing tomorrow morning."

"The earlier the better, My Lord! His Majesty received the news with a burst of grief, and there is

nobody he prefers to have with him in such trying
circumstances as yourself."

The Marquis received the compliment somewhat
wryly. He knew how emotional the new King could be.

All through his life he had over-dramatised every
situation from the time when at the age of twenty-two he
had stabbed himself in a frenzy because he was determined to make Mrs. Fitzherbert marry him.

Since then he had on every possible occasion
resorted to hysterical outbursts or floods of tears to
express himself.

As the Marquis poured Mr. Bingham a glass of
champagne from the bottle resting in a silver wine-
cooler, he thought that the King's over-dramatisation of
his father's death was the last thing he wanted at this
particular moment, and that made him remember Cara.

If he had to go to London, what was he to do about
her?

And what was more, how was he to announce his
marriage to his friends?

Something the Marquis hated more than anything
else was any scandal connected with himself. Yet, for the
moment he could not imagine how he could present to
the Social World the fact that he had a wife whom
nobody had seen or heard of before.

He knew it would be as startling in its own way as
was the death of the King.

However, as the thoughts raced through his mind
he appeared quite calm, as having handed Mr. Bingham
a glass of champagne he poured one out for himself.

As he picked up the glass he realised that his visitor
was not drinking but was looking at him in a speculative
way, as if he waited for him to make a move.

The Marquis understood what was expected of him.

He lifted his glass to say slowly and distinctly:

"The King! God bless him!"

"The King!" Mr. Bingham repeated, and drank the
champagne as if he was sorely in need of sustenance.

A little later the Marquis, having instructed the Butler to show Mr. Bingham to his room, went upstairs and, turning towards the South Wing, walked quickly towards his bedroom, knowing that his valet would have a bath waiting for him.

While he bathed he wanted to think over this new problem which made it impossible now for him to stay in the country as he had intended to do.

He had almost reached his own room when from out of a doorway ahead of him appeared Mrs. Peel.

As he saw her the Marquis knew without being told that Cara had been moved into the room next to his.

This meant that the whole household was now aware of his marriage, she was being treated as his wife, and she would in future sleep, as was traditional at Broome, in the Marchioness's bedroom.

For a moment he felt a surge of anger that they should have anticipated his instructions and, what was more, put Cara in a bedroom that had not been occupied since his mother had died.

If he could have obeyed his impulse he would have thrown Cara out to sleep in the attics or anywhere, as long as it was not close to him.

Then as Mrs. Peel curtseyed to him respectfully, once again his self-control made him acknowledge her and listen expressionlessly as she said:

"Her Ladyship seems a little better, M'Lord, and although at first I did think of asking Your Lordship to send for a Physician to look at Her Ladyship's back, I do not now think it will be necessary."

The Marquis stiffened.

He was well aware that if the local Physician examined Cara it would be impossible for him to keep to himself the fact that the new Marchioness of Broome had been beaten until the blood flowed, and chattering tongues would carry the story from one end of the County to the other.

"I have no wish, Mrs. Peel," he said in his most

commanding voice, "for anybody to be aware of Her Ladyship's injuries, and I trust you to see that it is not spoken of either inside the house or outside!"

"I'll do my best, M'Lord," Mrs. Peel replied.

She curtseyed again as the Marquis walked past her to open the door of his own room, and having passed inside to close it in a manner that was suspiciously like a slam.

Mrs. Peel gave a little sigh and walked away down the passage.

The Marquis would have been surprised if he had known how distressed and upset she was that he should have been married in such a strange, unaccountable manner, and to a young lady who not only had been ill-treated in a way she found appalling, but who was also not the type of lady she had expected to welcome as the Marquis's wife.

"Short hair and trousers!" Mrs. Peel murmured to herself as she moved towards the other part of the house. "What's the world coming to, I ask myself?"

The Marquis and Mr. Bingham dined together and discussed discreetly what would happen now that after waiting for so many years the Regent was at last on the throne.

"I can only hope, Mr. Bingham," the Marquis said, "that His Majesty will listen, as the Prime Minister and the Cabinet will not, to my continual demands for some sort of reform before it is too late."

Mr. Bingham, who was an intelligent man, shook his head.

"Things are getting worse in the North, My Lord," he replied, "but unfortunately everybody in power seems to think that if they ignore what is occurring, the menace of it will go away."

The Marquis's lips tightened.

He knew that the measures known as the "Six Acts," by which the Government was endeavouring to curb the activities of the Revolutionaries, had only made things worse.

He thought too that letters like the one from the Duke of Cambridge, who said that "nothing but firmness" could quell the "abominable revolutionary spirit now prevalent in England," were just a lot of "hot air."

He had in fact spoken to the Regent very firmly, telling him that something must be done, and His Royal Highness had been made personally aware of the necessity when hissed by an immense mob outside his own front door.

Lady Hertford, his latest fancy, had been all but pitched out of her chair into the street and had to be rescued by the Bow Street Runners.

"What is wanted," he said aloud "is cheaper food, higher wages, and somebody to make the working people feel that their problems are understood."

"I am sure His Majesty would become aware of what is required if Your Lordship would explain it to him," Mr. Bingham said.

The Marquis knew that the new Monarch, beset by problems of his own, the most notable being the behaviour of his wife, the Princess Caroline, would find it hard to listen.

The more he thought of the King's unhappy marriage, the more he was reminded of Cara lying upstairs at the moment.

Ever since the Princess's arrival from Brunswick in August 1814, Caroline had been providing Europe with scandal after scandal.

She had dressed her gentlemen in a startling new livery of gaudily embroidered coats and plumed hats.

At Genoa she had appeared at a Ball dressed *en Venses,* or rather not dressed above the waist.

At Baden she had pranced at the *Opera of the Widowed Margraviere* into the box shouting with laughter and wearing an outlandish peasant's head-dress ornamented with candles and flapping ribbons.

At Genoa she had driven through the streets in a glittering mother-of-pearl Phaeton, dressed in pink and white like a little girl, and showing a large expanse of middle-aged bosom and two stout legs in pink top-boots.

At Naples at a Ball she was alleged to have appeared *"in a most indecent manner, her breasts and arms being entirely naked."*

In Athens she had *"appeared almost naked and danced with her servants."*

One by one these incidents, which had lost nothing in the telling, flashed through the Marquis's mind.

With horror he saw himself suffering in the same way from his wife, and having people say, as Lady Bessborough had:

"Having seen the Princess at a Ball, I cannot tell you how sorry and ashamed I felt as an Englishwoman."

Although he did not talk about it, the Marquis was exceedingly proud of his heritage.

His ancestors were part of the history of England, and the Bromleys, which was the family name, had played their part not only in attendance at Court but on every notable battlefield whether on land or on sea.

He himself had been very careful never to do anything that would defame or dishonour the coat-of-arms which was carved over the front door of Broome and which decorated his carriages in London.

Then he told himself, as if he must soothe down the temper rising within him, that Cara, even though she had appeared dressed in an indecent manner, and with her hair cut in order to run away, was only a child compared to the plump, over-boisterous Princess Caroline.

It was ridiculous for him to think that he could not make a girl of eighteen behave properly in the future and obey him.

"After all, I have had command of a great number of troops," he consoled himself.

But he had the uncomfortable feeling that a woman,

whatever her age, could be more difficult than a whole Battalion of men who were trained to take orders.

He went on talking to Mr. Bingham, and when at last the Courtier retired to bed, saying that he would like as much sleep as possible, knowing how many duties awaited him in London, the Marquis knew he must advise Cara of this sudden but unavoidable change in his plans.

He supposed she would not be well enough to travel tomorrow, but he had no wish to leave her for long on her own at Broome.

Although it might be awkward in London, he had the uneasy feeling that it would be best for her to be near him so that he would know what she was doing and planning.

"She is my wife," he told himself, "and the sooner I make it clear that I will have no nonsense, the better!"

Having said good-night to Mr. Bingham, he walked down the passage to his own room.

He had looked at the large clock in the Hall before he ascended the stairs, and seeing that it was not yet ten, he thought there was no reason to suppose it was too late to disturb Cara.

One thing was perhaps a blessing in disguise. If the King was not to be acclaimed until Monday, it would certainly be a mistake for him to announce his marriage until after the Proclamation was over, so he might even delay it for several days.

"I shall wait until I am in London and see exactly what is happening," the Marquis thought.

He reached the door which led into the room where Cara was sleeping, then hesitated.

He decided it would be more natural if he came to her through the communicating door between their rooms with only a *Boudoir* between them.

This was the room in which his mother had spent much of her time. It was very feminine, being furnished with all the things the late Marchioness had particularly treasured: pictures of her son and daughters when they were children, a portrait of her husband on the wall, and some delightful paintings by French artists which the Marquis thought showed that her taste had been as good as his own.

As he entered the *Boudoir* from his own bedroom, having given his valet instructions to start packing immediately, he resented the fact that anybody should be using it, especially a wife he did not want.

He told himself that what was most important at the moment was that he should establish his relationship with Cara in a way which would leave her in no doubt as to who was the master and that she must behave as would be expected of his wife.

As usual, in accordance with the Marquis's orders, everything at Broome House was ready for immediate use, and the *Boudoir*, although he had not entered it since he had come home, was filled with flowers and the candles were lit.

This was something that happened every night when he was in residence, and although he had never opened the communicating door from the *Boudoir* into his own room, he was aware that everything was ready on the assumption that he might do so.

He felt now, however, with a darkening of his eyes, that the room had been prepared for Cara.

He deliberately did not glance at the portrait of his father over the mantelpiece or a very lovely one of his mother by Sir Joshua Reynolds on the other wall.

Instead he walked quickly towards the door opposite his own, which led into the bedroom.

For a moment as he put out his hand to turn the handle he had a feeling of revulsion, and every instinct in his body cried out against the woman who had taken his much-valued freedom from him.

Then he told himself it had not been her fault, and it would be an unsportsmanlike gesture to blame her entirely for what had occurred.

He turned the handle, only to find that the door was locked, then turned it again to make quite certain he was not mistaken.

Because he could not believe that Cara would deliberately lock him out or anticipate that he might wish to see her, he thought that by some stupid lapse on the part of a housemaid, the door must have been left locked even after the bedroom was occupied.

He debated with himself whether he should go into the passage and try the other door, then instead he decided to knock.

He raised his hand and knocked on the wooden panel, not loudly, for he had no wish for his valet, who was in his bedroom, to know what was happening, but loud enough for anybody inside to hear.

There was silence and he knocked again.

"Cara!"

For a moment he thought that she had not heard him, but after a moment she replied:

"What is . . . it?"

"I want to talk to you. Open the door!"

There was a pause. Then she said distinctly:

"No!"

"It is important that I should speak to you," the Marquis insisted.

There was no reply, and he thought perhaps she was getting out of bed and coming to the door. When she spoke again, he was sure that was what had happened because her voice sounded nearer.

"What do you want to see me about?" she asked.

"My plans have changed, and I have to tell you about them."

"You can tell me through the door."

The Marquis felt his temper rising.

"Stop being ridiculous," he said sharply. "I can hardly talk to you through a closed and locked door."

"Why not?"

"Because it is foolish and unnecessary."

"I have gone to bed . . . I want to sleep."

"I can understand that," the Marquis said patiently. "But I still want to speak to you. I am your husband."

"I know, but I have no wish to talk to you at this hour of the night."

"It may be late," the Marquis agreed, "but I was told earlier that you were asleep, and I am leaving for London first thing tomorrow morning."

He thought she was considering what he had said.

"Open the door, Cara!" he ordered. "I will tell you what has happened."

"No!"

The monosyllable had a very final ring about it.

The Marquis resisted an impulse, which was very unlike him, to put his shoulder against the door and break the lock.

"I insist on your doing what I tell you to do," he said. "It is important that you should know why I am going to London."

"You can leave me a note," Cara said, "unless you wish me to accompany you. But I do not think I shall be well enough."

"No. I was not going to suggest that," the Marquis answered, "but it will be necessary for you to join me in a day or so."

"Very well," Cara replied. "When I am better I will try to carry out your instructions."

As she spoke, the Marquis heard her voice fading away and knew without being told that she had moved back to the bed.

He could hardly believe that she was deliberately disobeying him and ignoring his request.

But a moment later he heard her voice in the distance as she said: "Good-night, My Lord!" and knew that their conversation, if that was what it could be called, was at an end.

* * *

Mrs. Peel did not bring Cara's breakfast to her the following morning until some hours after the Marquis had left for London.

Propped against the silver-crested dish which covered a plate of Crown Derby china was a letter inscribed with a strong, upright handwriting. Cara thought she would have recognised it as belonging to the Marquis wherever she had seen it.

It was, she thought, characteristic of him: authoritative, determined, and, in a way, overwhelming.

Deliberately, because she thought it would annoy him if he knew, she ate her breakfast before she read it.

Because she felt very much better than she had the night before, she enjoyed the eggs and the fresh country butter from the Marquis's Jersey cows, which she spread with home-made quince jam, a specialty of the Broome Still-Room.

Only when she had eaten almost everything that was on the tray did she pick up the Marquis's note and open it.

It stated, without any preliminary:

"His Majesty King George III died on Saturday evening. The new King will be proclaimed today and requires my presence. I am therefore going to London and will be at Broome House in Park Lane.

If you are well enough, I suggest that you join me tomorrow or the next day, as apart from the fact that I think you should be with me when I announce our marriage, you will require clothes which can only be provided for you in London.

If you will inform Mr. Curtis, who is in charge of the household, on which day you are prepared to travel, he will make all the arrangements for your comfort, and also for a maid to travel with you."

I. B.

The Marquis had not signed his letter but merely added his initials entwined at the bottom of the page.

Cara read what he had written, then read it again.

She was interested to learn that the King was dead, and she thought that after waiting so long the new King would be thrilled and delighted at being at last on the throne and having the power to do as he wished.

'If I were King I would abolish matrimony,' Cara thought, with only herself in mind.

Then she remembered, as the Marquis had done, that the King was married to a woman who had humiliated him by her behaviour and had become a laughing-stock not only in England but in Europe.

Some of her uncle's friends had met Princess Caroline when they had been abroad, and they had talked about her behaviour interspersed with roars of laughter, which Cara had thought was insulting not only to her husband, the Regent, but also to the English people.

"I wish you could have seen her, Lionel," one of her uncle's friends had said, "when after her English attendants had left her she filled their places with a collection of French chamber-maids and cooks, Arab footboys, Austrian postillions, and Italian footmen!"

"Good God!" the Earl had ejaculated. "Is that true?"

"They are overbearing, and their insolence is beyond description," his friend replied, "and their entrance into any territory is as much regretted as an incursion of free-booters."

"I hope His Royal Highness knows this," the Earl sniggered.

"You may be quite certain that somebody will tell him," his friend replied. "I heard that he swore like a trooper when he heard how his wife had ridden into Jerusalem on an ass."

The way they were talking made Cara feel not only

embarrassed but as if she too was humiliated as the Regent would be.

She had learnt that her uncle hated the Regent and gloried in hearing anything about Princess Caroline that was degrading and derogatory.

It struck her that the Marquis would doubtless expect the same kind of behaviour from her because she was her uncle's niece.

'I hate him because he is my husband,' she thought. 'At the same time, Papa and Mama would expect me to behave like a lady, whatever Uncle Lionel is like.'

Because her back was still very painful, she decided it would be foolish to go to London to join the Marquis until she felt very much stronger.

If she was horrified and angry at finding herself married to him, she knew that his feelings at being married to her would be equally violent.

She had not heard her uncle deriding him and disparaging him as the owner of successful race-horses without knowing that in character the Marquis was everything that the Earl was not.

At the same time, he was a man, and she had no wish to be married to any man. More than anything else, she was concerned with considering if she would break the marriage.

If not, she must try in some way, however difficult it might be, to escape to an independence where she would belong to no man and could be herself.

It was not going to be easy, she was well aware of that, and as the day progressed she learnt, and it infuriated her, that the Marquis was having her carefully guarded in case she should make an attempt to run away from him as she had done from her uncle.

She realised he was perceptive enough to know that she had no interest in the social position she had attained on becoming his wife, and she was still intent on either reaching France, where she could be with her friend, or on disappearing.

She did not ask herself how she knew that the Marquis was thinking this, but because she was intuitive she felt quite certain that this was the truth, and that without saying anything to her he had made it impossible for any form of escape from Broome to take place.

Explanations were offered, and very plausible ones, for her guards.

"I thought you might want something in the night, M'Lady,' Mrs. Peel said, "so I have told Robinson to sleep in your dressing-room next door. You only have to call out and she will be at your side within moments."

"Thank you," Cara said, but she had known at once why Robinson, an elderly housemaid, was there.

On the third day she decided she would join the Marquis in London and when she went downstairs was not surprised to find that she was to journey not only with Robinson but also with Mr. Curtis.

He travelled with her in the coach, sitting beside her on the back seat, while Robinson, looking exactly as a lady's-maid should in a black bonnet and wrapped in a heavy black cape, sat opposite them.

Mrs. Peel had excelled herself in finding an elegant travelling-gown that Cara could wear for the journey to London.

It was extremely becoming and had a very pretty coat that went with it, heavily trimmed with sable, with a small muff to match.

"Who could have left these pretty things behind?" she asked Mrs. Peel.

"They belong to His Lordship's younger sister, M'Lady, who is now abroad in a hot climate and has no need of furs. I'm sure she won't mind Your Ladyship borrowing them. Later I'll put them back in moth-balls to keep them safe until her return."

There was no mention of what had happened to the Eton suit in which Cara had arrived at Broome, and she was too shy to ask Mrs. Peel what she had done with it.

She thought with a little twist of her lips that

perhaps it would be kept in Mrs. Peel's wardrobe for some youth in the future who might be short of just such an outfit.

The bonnet with which Mrs. Peel provided her was definitely not as fashionable as those Cara had seen in London, but it was quite pretty.

The seamstress who worked in the house had added a few ostrich-feathers from another source to make it more suitable for the new Marchioness of Broome.

Because she could not prevent herself from being curious, Cara asked Mrs. Peel before she left:

"How did you know, or did he tell you, that I was married to His Lordship?"

For a moment Mrs. Peel seemed disconcerted, then she said:

"Your Ladyship must be aware that little goes on in the house without Mr. Newman or myself being aware of it."

"I suppose that is the same in any big house," Cara said with a smile.

Because of the way Mrs. Peel had mentioned the Butler, Cara was sure that every word her uncle had said in the Breakfast-Room had been listened to outside the door.

And the fact that they had gone straight to the Chapel only confirmed that the servants had overheard while eavesdropping.

She did not know until she arrived in London that the Marquis, intent on attending His Majesty, had been furious when he opened the morning newspapers to find that the Earl, determined to have the last say, had sent an announcement of their marriage to *The Gazette*.

However, he had no time to express his anger before he hurried to Carlton House to stand in the cold air beside the King, the Royal Dukes, and Prince Leopold, and listen to the aged Garter King of Arms read out the traditional formula of accession in a slow and quavering voice.

The next day the new King had inflammation of the lungs, and a bulletin was issued with the grave news that His Majesty was severely indisposed.

The Marquis visited Carlton House to find that the King could not sleep, had a racing pulse, pains in the chest, and great difficulty in breathing.

On Wednesday he was close to death, and everybody walked about speaking in whispers.

The Princess de Lieven, who always had something pertinent to say on such occasions, said to the Marquis:

"If he should die, Shakespeare's tragedies would pale before such a catastrophe. Father and son in the past have been buried together, but two Kings? I hope this one will recover."

"I hope so indeed!" the Marquis agreed in a heart-felt voice, wondering if he died whether the Queen would make an attempt to be accepted as Regent.

The idea was so horrifying that he was disliking Cara more than ever when on returning to Broome House he was told that she had arrived.

Because he had been thinking of her in the image of Queen Caroline, he was expecting her to be large-bosomed, red-faced, and truculent.

But when he entered the Drawing-Room, where he was told she was waiting for him, he found it difficult for the moment to recognise her.

As he approached, she rose from the chair in which she had been sitting, and he saw how very small she was, and her hair curling on top of her head seemed to hold the sunshine.

Her eyes seemed enormous as they turned up at the corners and were not in the least aggressive.

She curtseyed, and the Marquis bowed formally, then looked down at her. As he did so, he realised with a shock of genuine surprise that she was frightened of him.

Chapter Five

Women had looked at the Marquis in many different ways—with love, desire, jealousy, anger, and reproach—but he could not remember any woman before looking at him with an expression of physical fear.

For the first time since his marriage he was thinking not of his own outraged feelings but of Cara's, and he realised that the punishment she had received from her uncle had been enough to terrify any young woman and make her afraid of all men.

Without a great deal of difficulty he forced himself to smile at her in a way that most women had found irresistible.

"Are you better?" he asked.

"Yes, thank you," Cara replied. "I waited until I felt well enough to travel."

"That was sensible," the Marquis said. "And now that you are here, we have a great deal to talk about. Suppose we both sit down?"

He noticed that Cara did so carefully, as if her back was still stiff, and that she sat upright on the edge of the chair, with her hands in her lap.

As he sat down opposite her he saw that the expression in her strange eyes was still wary and there was an undoubted touch of fear in their green-gold depths

The Marquis had meant to start by telling her about the King and the anxiety his illness was causing both at Court and in the country.

Instead, because he was curious, he asked:

"Has your uncle often beaten you?"

Cara looked away from him and there was just a faint touch of colour in her cheeks as if she was embarrassed.

"Whenever I have annoyed him," she replied.

"It is intolerable that he should have treated you in such a manner!" the Marquis ejaculated.

"He hates me because he hated Papa!" Cara said simply.

"Why should he hate your father?"

There was a little pause before Cara answered:

"My father was the elder son, and Uncle Lionel was, I think, desperately jealous of his position as soon as he was old enough to understand it."

The Marquis did not speak, and after a moment she went on:

"Papa was in every way different from my uncle. He was a sportsman, brave, kind, and everybody loved him, just as they . . . loathe Uncle Lionel!"

There was a sudden violence in her voice, which told the Marquis very clearly what she too felt for the Earl.

"Perhaps it would be easier for us both," he said, "if you would explain to me a little about your family and how your uncle became your Guardian. I presume that not only your father but also your mother is dead?"

Cara nodded.

"Mama died . . . last year."

"And your father?"

"He died five years ago. Two days before he would have inherited the title from my grandfather."

As she spoke there was a note in her voice that was so strange that the Marquis looked at her enquiringly, and when she did not elaborate, he remarked:

"I feel that there is some mystery about your father's death."

Cara looked at him swiftly, as if she was surprised that he should be so intuitive, but when she did not reply the Marquis said:

"I think, Cara, the most important thing in trying to make our strange marriage work smoothly is for us to be absolutely frank with each other, and that is something I am prepared to be with you."

"Very well," Cara replied, "if you want the truth, I believe, although I cannot prove it, that my uncle . . . murdered Papa!"

Her words were a shock, even though the Marquis thought he might have anticipated them.

Then he told himself that Cara, in making the accusation, was influenced by her personal hatred of her uncle.

In a quiet and calm voice, which those who consulted him politically would have recognised, the Marquis said:

"Suppose you tell me exactly what happened?"

As Cara began to speak, his eyes were on her face as if he was minutely weighing everything she said, to be quite certain whether it was true or false.

Cara gave a little sigh before she began:

"We all lived, Papa, Mama, and I, in the big house which the Matlocks have owned for two hundred years. Grandpapa liked us to be there with him because otherwise he would have been very lonely, and in fact he loved Papa very much."

She paused before she said in a voice that told the Marquis she was speaking more to herself than to him:

"We were very . . . very . . . happy."

"Then what happened?" the Marquis prompted.

"Grandpapa became ill, and although Uncle Lionel never came home except when he wanted money, Papa thought it only right that he should inform his brother that the Doctors thought that Grandpapa might die."

The way she spoke told the Marquis how worried and distressed they all had been.

"I had not seen Uncle Lionel for some years," Cara went on, "and I suppose that because now I was older, the moment he appeared I knew exactly what he was like. I knew too that he was planning how much he could obtain for himself if Grandpapa died, and how much he loathed Papa for being the heir."

"Did your father realise this?" the Marquis enquired.

"Papa had always tried to help Uncle Lionel and had even given him money, which we could ill afford, to help him meet his debts."

"I presume he was in debt on this occasion?"

"Very deeply, as we were to learn afterwards, when he sold everything in the house that was not entailed."

Cara thought the Marquis looked surprised, and she explained:

"That was after Papa was dead and he inherited."

"How did that happen?"

"Two days before Grandpapa died, when we all knew there was no hope of saving him, Papa and Uncle Lionel went out riding together . . . but he returned alone."

For a moment it was difficult for her to continue. Then she forced herself to say:

"According to Uncle Lionel, they had both taken a very high fence, but Papa's horse had fallen, throwing him to the ground so heavily that he broke his neck."

"But you did not believe it was an accident?"

"Papa was a brilliant rider and knew every fence and every jump on the Estate. He would never have let his horse attempt anything that was too high!"

"Why should you suspect that your uncle was responsible for his death?" the Marquis enquired.

"Papa was brought home on a gate carried by farm-workers," Cara answered, "and it was a long time later in the evening when I asked Uncle Lionel about

Papa's horse, which was the favourite he always rode and with which he had never had any difficulty."

"What had happened to it?"

"Uncle Lionel said that the fall had broken its leg and he had therefore shot it."

The way she spoke told the Marquis without any further words exactly what she suspected. He knew that if a man was wicked and unscrupulous enough to shoot a horse at the moment when it was taking a high jump, the result must be a precipitate fall which could quite easily kill its rider.

There was silence before the Marquis asked:

"Could you really accuse your uncle of such a dastardly crime?"

"Mama thought, as I did, that that was what he had done," Cara answered, "but she said that accusations would not bring Papa back to life, and it would only make things between us much more unpleasant than they were already."

Cara drew in her breath before she finished:

"Also, we were completely dependent financially upon Uncle Lionel. Papa had no money of his own, although Grandpapa had made him an allowance in the same way as he made one to his other son!"

She paused, as if she was thinking back, before she went on:

"Because agriculture had suffered during the war when so many men were away fighting with Wellington's Army or at sea, we had not had good harvests, and the tenants were behind with their rents so that we too had to make very strict economies."

"I think things are the same throughout the country," the Marquis said, "and I can understand that it meant your mother had no money in hand."

"We had practically nothing," Cara replied. "Uncle Lionel turned us out of the big house and gave us a small cottage on the Estate. He would barely furnish it, and he allowed us to have nothing that was of any value."

The Marquis could understand that this had been very humiliating.

"Fortunately," Cara continued, "Mama could prove that Grandpapa had given her two of the horses as presents, one at Christmas and one on her birthday, so at least we had something to ride."

She looked at the Marquis as if she thought he must know how important that was, then went on:

"Uncle Lionel closed the country house and went to London. He sacked the servants, refused to give them pensions, and behaved in a manner which made me ashamed of my own family."

The Marquis thought it was the type of behaviour he would expect of the Earl.

But there was no point in saying so, and he was concentrating on learning what had happened to Cara.

"This must have been in about 1815," he said aloud.

It was the year the war had ended, and he had still been on the Continent, following Wellington's victory at Waterloo.

"There was a great deal of hardship and often hunger when the men began to come home after they had been dismissed from the Forces," Cara said, "but Mama was more concerned with seeing that I was given a good education."

Her voice softened as she continued:

"Fortunately, she had a few pieces of jewellery which Papa had given her over the years. These she sold so that I could have the best Teachers available in the neighbourhood, but it meant we had to live very frugally and could not afford extravagances of any sort."

Now there was a new note of aggression in her voice, and the Marquis understood that she did not want pity, least of all from him.

She was telling her story exactly as it had happened, which was what he had asked her to do.

He did not speak, but his grey eyes were on her face, which was very expressive as she went on:

"Then last year Mama became ill. She had always been very unhappy without Papa, and although it was an agony for her to leave me, I knew she would be happy again once she was with him."

The Marquis felt that this statement was very revealing as to Cara's beliefs, and he thought how few of the women he knew were religious enough to have faith in an "after-life" where the man they loved was waiting for them.

"After Mama was buried," Cara continued in a different manner altogether, "Uncle Lionel arrived."

"You had not seen him for some time?"

"No, not since he had closed the house, and I had been only thirteen at the time."

Now there was something like horror in her voice as she said:

"As soon as he came into the cottage, I realised he was surprised by my appearance and that I looked different from what he had expected."

"You mean that he admired you?" the Marquis interposed.

"What I knew," Cara answered, "and I cannot tell you why I knew it, was that he thought my looks might be useful to him. I hated him as Papa's murderer, and now I was afraid for myself in a way I cannot explain."

"Did he say you were to live with him?"

"He ordered me to pack what clothes I had and come with him to London," Cara replied, "and I had no choice but to obey him."

"When did this happen?" the Marquis enquired.

"Just before Christmas, and as we drove away he said:

" 'You will not wear mourning for your mother, and I want no weeping and wailing in my house. The only asset you have is that you are of marriageable age, and I will find a suitable husband for you.' "

"What did you reply?"

"I told him I had no intention of marrying any man unless I loved him."

"I suppose your defiance annoyed him."

"He struck me!" Cara answered. "And when we reached his house in Grosvenor Square in London, and I repeated what I had already said, he . . . beat me with a whip!"

The expression on her face told the Marquis what a horrifying experience it had been, but she went on quickly:

"There was nothing I could do. He bought me some gowns, having said that everything I owned was fit only for the rag-bag. I tried to think of how I could possibly escape, but I had not a penny to call my own."

The Marquis looked puzzled, knowing that she had told him she had twenty pounds in the pocket of her coat, and also some jewellery.

"I knew that it was hopeless to run away without being able to pay my way," Cara went on, "and until Christmas came there was no chance of my possessing even a shilling."

"What happened at Christmas?"

"A friend of my uncle's came to stay at Grosvenor Square, and she was very rich."

"What was her name?"

"She called herself *La Marchesa* di Cesari," Cara said, "but I found out from the servants that she was nothing of the sort. She was a singer who was always under the protection of rich men, and she had the most fantastic jewellery, besides being very generous with her money."

The Marquis was beginning to see the whole story, which had puzzled him, falling into place like the pieces of a jig-saw puzzle.

He listened intently as Cara went on:

"The *Marchesa* was impressed by Uncle Lionel because he had a title, and he was enamoured, or pretended to be, of her."

"It was hardly the right sort of society for you to be in," the Marquis remarked. "I am quite sure your mother would not have approved."

"At first I was not allowed to attend the parties they gave," Cara replied. "Then one night the *Marchesa*, who was really quite a kindly woman, said to Uncle Lionel:

"'Oh, let the child have a bit of fun. After all, Christmas festivities were meant for children.'

"I found it exciting to go downstairs in a pretty gown for the party," Cara continued, "although the guests were a strange collection and I think Mama would have been shocked not only by the women but also by the men."

She paused before she added:

"And . . . most especially by . . . Sir Mortimer Forstrath."

The Marquis remembered that he had intended to make enquiries about that particular gentleman, but the new King's illness had put it our of his head.

"That was the man your uncle wanted you to marry," he said.

"The moment I saw him he made me creep!" Cara replied. "I did not like the way he looked at me, and when he touched me it gave me 'goose-pimples.' I felt, as the servants say, 'as if a ghost was walking over my grave.'"

"What was wrong with him?"

"I did not know what it was that made him so repulsive right from the start," Cara answered. "Then Emily, the maid who looked after me and had grown fond of me, told me about him."

"What did she say?"

Cara's voice dropped almost to a whisper as she replied:

"She said . . . that he went frequently to a wicked house that . . . belonged to a Mrs. Barclay . . . where gentlemen like him paid large sums of money . . . to whip . . . young girls."

The Marquis stiffened and looked at Cara incredulously.

He knew whom she was talking about and was well aware that Mrs. Barclay's house of ill-repute was notorious.

It was the sort of place he would never visit himself, but the fact that the woman had made a fortune out of debauched and usually elderly men who liked such exotic pleasures was well known in the Clubs of St. James's.

"How can the maid-servant possibly have told you about such things?" he asked.

"Emily was worried about me," Cara replied, "and she had heard about Sir Mortimer from Uncle Lionel's valet. He also told her that Sir Mortimer was prepared to pay ten thousand pounds to Uncle Lionel if he would permit him to marry me."

The Marquis understood now why that particular sum had been extorted from him by the Earl.

It seemed utterly incredible that any man who called himself a gentleman could sink to such a level of obscenity, and he thought that his dislike of the Earl of Matlock, which had existed ever since he first knew him, was certainly justified.

"Now you can . . . understand," Cara said in a small voice, "why I ran . . . away."

"And to do so you took jewellery and money belonging to the *Marchesa!*"

"I helped her up to bed after her Birthday Party, which went on until the early hours of the morning," Cara said. "I was allowed to be present because Sir Mortimer wanted me there, but I had a miserable time trying to avoid him."

Her voice sharpened as she said:

"At one moment I thought of stabbing him with a knife. Then I knew I would doubtless fail to kill him and the result would simply be that I would receive another beating from Uncle Lionel, who had grown more and more violent every time I said I would never . . . never marry such a man!"

"So you stole the *Marchesa's* jewellery while you were helping her to bed!"

"Her lady's-maid was downstairs, enjoying herself with the rest of the staff," Cara answered. "Most of Uncle Lionel's servants behaved in a manner that neither Papa nor Grandpapa would have allowed. Mama always said that 'a bad master breeds bad servants.'"

"That is true," the Marquis agreed. "So you put the *Marchesa* to bed and took her jewellery."

"Not the jewels she was wearing, that would have been very stupid! But when I put them away in her big jewel-box, I saw at the bottom of it two pieces she never wore, and as you know, I still have them."

"I had forgotten that," the Marquis said. "They must certainly be returned to their rightful owner. I can hardly allow you as my wife to be prosecuted for being a thief!"

Cara's eyes widened before she said:

"Uncle Lionel would be delighted if I was hanged for such a crime! Please let me give you the jewellery. I am sure you can think of some clever way of returning it to the *Marchesa* without her being aware that it is missing."

Then, before the Marquis could agree, she gave a little cry and said:

"Emily would do that for me if I could get in touch with her."

"We will consider it carefully," the Marquis said, "but first finish your story."

"I took the brooch and the collet to my room and hid them," Cara said, "and the next day the *Marchesa* was very ill, too ill to get up. She asked me to fetch her a handkerchief from one of the drawers, and while I was doing so I saw that she had a great amount of money thrown there untidily amongst her other things."

Cara looked a little embarrassed as she explained:

"I knew it was what she had won at the party and when she had been gambling with Uncle Lionel at one of the places they often visited in Mayfair."

There were a number of Gaming Houses, as the Marquis knew, that catered only for the aristocrats and which were therefore considered private houses and outside the jurisdiction of the Gaming Laws.

"I was quite certain she had not counted it and could have no idea of how much she had won," Cara went on. "She was very stupid about English money and always said she could not understand what any of our coinage meant."

"So you helped yourself!" the Marquis said drily.

"It was either that or stay and marry Sir Mortimer! Uncle Lionel had already told me he was arranging for our marriage to take place within two weeks, and I was to order for myself a wedding-gown."

"Now I understand why you decided to run away, and perhaps in the circumstances it was the best thing you could do."

For the first time during this conversation Cara's eyes twinkled.

"Are you really approving of something I have done, My Lord?" she enquired mockingly.

The Marquis laughed.

"You are leaving me no other alternative."

"I had found the Eton suit in the attic earlier when I had been exploring the house," Cara said. "There were several there, and I think they must have belonged to Papa or Uncle Lionel when they were boys. There were also costumes which were at least a century old."

"The attics of every house in London are full of treasures," the Marquis said. "I know my mother once found a gown at Broome that had real diamonds sewn on it, and it had been in the attic for a hundred years!"

"I shall certainly have a treasure-hunt if I return there!" Cara exclaimed.

The Marquis realised that she had said "if" instead of "when."

As she was aware that he had noticed the slip, she said quickly:

"I want to talk to you about that."

"Yes, of course," he said, "but may I say first, Cara, I am glad I have heard the whole story of your attempted escape from your uncle, and I can understand now why you felt it imperative to do so."

"I am afraid it was unfortunate for you that I chose your travelling-chariot because it had six horses," Cara said, "but I suspect that whoever it was who saw me climb into it and told Uncle Lionel, the result, as far as I am concerned, would have been the same."

It flashed through the Marquis's mind that she might not have chosen either such a rich man who could be blackmailed into marrying her, or, from the Earl's point of view, an enemy over whom he could score such a satisfying revenge.

But there was no point in saying so, and after a pause he said:

"What is done cannot be undone, and I hope, Cara, that we are both intelligent enough to make the best of what for us both is an unfortunate situation."

"Surely it is possible for you to break the marriage?" Cara asked. "After all, Uncle Lionel blackmailed you into it."

"Nevertheless, we were legally married by Special License and by a Parson," the Marquis replied.

Because he resented it so much, he had no idea how his voice altered when he spoke, and became cold, sharp, and contemptuous.

"I have a . . . suggestion to . . . make," Cara said in a very small voice.

"What is it?"

"If you had no wish to be married . . . neither had I, and if I . . . . disappear when after a year or two you

will be able to . . . assume that I am . . . dead, you will
be free."

"If that idea was practical I suppose we might
consider it," the Marquis said. "But you must be aware
that if you disappeared, your uncle would undoubtedly
accuse me of having murdered you and create such a
scandal that the whole country would be searching for
you."

Cara looked at him with startled eyes.

"Do you really think Uncle Lionel would do that?"

"I am sure of it," the Marquis said, "if for no other
reason that he could then force me to pay him to keep
silent!"

"I hate him! I hate him!" Cara said furiously. "How
can he be allowed to flourish in his wickedness? I am
sure he killed Papa, and perhaps a great number of other
people, for all we know!"

"Such suppositions are quite useless without proof,"
the Marquis said coldly.

"What can I do?"

"The answer is quite simple," he replied. "You are
my wife, and it should not be difficult for you to behave
outwardly in the way the world will expect of anybody in
such a position."

Cara laughed.

"I am quite certain you know the answer to that,"
she said. "Why should I stay with somebody who hates
me because I am my uncle's niece?"

"I will try not to labour that point," the Marquis
promised, "since you are well aware that it would be
most unfair. You may be the niece of a man whom I
despise and am ready to condemn, but you are also the
daughter of your father and mother."

Cara rose from the chair in which she was sitting
and walked across the room to stand looking out the
window.

Outside was a small paved garden with, in the

centre, a very beautiful statue standing above a carved stone goldfish-pool.

Because it was winter there was no water in the pool, and in the garden itself there was no colour except for a few dwarf-sized shrubs which were evergreen.

Cara's eyes were looking at them, but actually she was considering her life with the Marquis and thinking that although it was unlikely he would beat her or physically ill-treat her as her uncle had done, it would be an existence without love.

She felt she could not face an atmosphere of hate and loneliness such as she had experienced while she was living in Grosvenor Square.

'I shall have to run away,' she thought. 'Whatever he may say, it is the only thing I can do.'

"What are you thinking, Cara?" the Marquis asked.

"At least my thoughts are my own!" she snapped.

"Perhaps I can guess them," he said. "I have a feeling you are still intent on leaving me. Let me make it quite clear that I will not allow you to do so."

Cara turned round to look at him.

"Why should you be so foolish," she said, "as to want me to stay when you know as well as I do that you will find my presence here intolerable? Every time you look at me you will remember how you have been humiliated by Uncle Lionel, and however much you try to forget, it will be a constant irritant that will make our lives a hell!"

The way she spoke was more surprising than what she actually said, and the Marquis rose from his chair to walk across the room and stand beside her.

She did not speak but merely stood looking up at him, her strange, slanting eyes seeming to hold a question which was impossible for him to answer.

He did not speak for a moment, then he said:

"You puzzle me, Cara, because you are quite unlike any young woman I have ever met before. But you constitute a problem which I have every intention of solving, and it would be far easier if we tried to solve it together."

"Now you are being very subtle," Cara said. "You want to get me on your side so that I shall obey you without actually realising I am doing so."

The Marquis laughed.

"In fact, I was thinking how uncomfortable it will be if we continue bickering and fighting from morning to night! I had thought when the war ended I had finished fighting enemies."

"I am not your enemy!" Cara flashed.

"No, that is true," he conceded, "and while I am quite prepared to fight with enemies outside the house, it would be an impossible situation if one very important one was inside."

"Now you are being conciliatory, and that, I feel sure, is far more dangerous than when you bristle aggressively and threaten me with every weapon within reach!"

The Marquis laughed again, and it was a spontaneous, whole-hearted sound.

"You certainly have a very unusual turn of phrase," he said. "I have a feeling, Cara, that as long as we can laugh, if not together, at least at ourselves, things will not be as black as they appear at the moment."

Cara looked away from him again into the garden, and the Marquis said:

"Because I have so much to do for His Majesty, who keeps demanding my presence at his bedside, could we for the moment call a truce?"

"I suppose we might do that," Cara conceded.

"Very well," the Marquis said with just a touch of satisfaction in his voice. "This is where you start by buying yourself a trousseau."

As he spoke he felt it would be impossible for any woman to refuse such a generous suggestion. In fact, he knew that any Beauty, in whatever strata of society she existed, would in the past have been wildly elated at such a suggestion coming from him.

But Cara appeared to be hesitating, and he could not understand why.

"I want my friends to admire my wife," he said, "and I think it extremely important from the point of view of both of us that they should believe we were married because we were attracted to each other, and not because we were compelled into it by your uncle."

"You do not think he will . . . tell everybody what really . . . happened?"

"I doubt it," the Marquis answered. "He has won what to him is a tremendous victory, and I think that while he will undoubtedly attack again, he will wait for the moment to see the result of what he has achieved so far."

Cara gave a little shiver.

"He . . . frightens me."

"Let me promise you one thing," the Marquis said. "Now that you are my wife, if he ever touches you again, I will kill him!"

The way he spoke without raising his voice was very impressive, and Cara turned to look at him with startled eyes.

"Do you . . . mean that?"

"I mean it!" the Marquis said positively. "I loathe and detest cruelty in any form! I am always prepared to mete out punishment to any man who ill-treats one of my horses, and I can only tell you that I am not speaking lightly when I say I would murder a man who frightened you."

Cara was looking at him wide-eyed, and he saw the colour come into her cheeks almost as if his reassurance had brought her to life.

Then she said:

"What you have just said . . . makes me feel safe for the first time since . . . Mama died."

"I assure you that you are completely and absolutely safe so long as you remain with me."

"Thank you," Cara said. "Thank you very much."

"I have been thinking," the Marquis went on, "that perhaps your uncle will realise his plan has misfired if he finds I am quite content with the situation he has created, and if I can convince my friends, who will be curious as to why we were married in such a strange manner, that it was something we did willingly because it was what we wanted to do."

Cara clasped her hands together.

"That is clever . . . very clever," she approved.

"I thought you would appreciate the subtlety of it," the Marquis said. "But we have to play our hands carefully to see what turns up, and be prepared to fight your uncle fairly and squarely when the occasion arises."

Cara nodded to show that she understood, and the Marquis went on:

"The first step is for you to look beautiful, because my friends will expect me to have married a beautiful woman, and secondly, in public at any rate, we must both appear happy in each other's company."

"You mean that it can be an act put on for Uncle Lionel's benefit, which he will find disconcerting," Cara said, as if she reasoned it out to herself.

"Exactly!" the Marquis agreed. "That is why I suggest that while I am busy in attendance upon the King, you buy yourself a trousseau that will make all the other women's eyes pop out with envy."

Again there was that unexpected little pause and he asked:

"What is troubling you?"

Cara looked up at him and said:

"I . . . I think perhaps I am being . . . very foolish but I have been so poor with Mama . . . and the only clothes I have owned were the ones she and I made together . . . and I am therefore afraid I would not have the . . . good taste or the . . . knowledge to choose the sort of clothes I should wear as . . . your wife."

The Marquis smiled and there was no need to force it to his lips.

"I understand what you are saying, Cara," he said, "and it was foolish of me not to know that was what you might feel. There is, however, a quite easy solution."

"What . . . is that?" Cara asked doubtfully.

"The dressmakers can come here, and we will choose your clothes together."

As he spoke, he thought how many gowns he had chosen not only for the mistresses whom he had kept in his comfortable house in Chelsea, but also for the Beauties who, while they loved him wholeheartedly, still expected to be able to dip their fingers into his large and generous purse.

They were always begging him for a gown for some special occasion, furs because they were cold, or perhaps a muff into which he could put his hand to warm their cold fingers.

After that there had been an avalanche of accessories to make them look beautiful in his eyes—bonnets to frame their gold, red, or raven-black hair, sunshades to protect their delicate white skins from sunburn, and of course jewels to embellish their long necks, their tiny shell-like ears, and their slender wrists.

'This at least will be the first time I have bought a trousseau for my own wife,' the Marquis thought.

Quite unexpectedly, he found it amusing.

Chapter Six

"They're reelly beautiful, M'Lady, they are reelly!" Emily said in awe-struck tones as Cara showed her the clothes that had arrived daily from the dressmakers.

She thought the same herself, and she was honest enough to acknowledge that it was due to the Marquis that all the garments which had been made for her were so glamorous and alluring, for she would not have had either the experience or the good taste to know exactly what suited her.

She lifted down from the wardrobe a gown in pale green which matched her eyes, and when she held it up against her Emily exclaimed:

"It makes you look like a bit o' spring, M'Lady, and that's the truth!"

Because she was curious about what was going on at her uncle's house in Grosvenor Square since she had left it, Cara had been pleased when she was told that Emily had called to see her.

"It might seem a bit presumptuous, M'Lady," Emily had said humbly, "but I've wondered about you ever since you runs away, and the master was so furious he were like a madman 'til Tim said as how he'd seen you gettin' into a chariot outside Carlton House."

"So it was Tim who saw me!" Cara exclaimed.

Tim was the scullery-boy who she had always

thought was rather a tiresome character and not quite normal.

He could be shrewd when it suited him, but the servants disliked him because he was spiteful and often told tales about them to the Earl.

"Yes, 'twas Tim right enough," Emily said. "He's always going to Carlton House to watch the Gentry going in and out, just as he watches the houses in the Square. I often wonders why it interests him."

In a way, Cara was glad to learn who had been watching her.

She had lain awake sometimes wondering how she could have been so unfortunate as to have attracted anybody's attention when she slipped into the Marquis's chariot, hoping that she had escaped from her uncle forever.

Although she still played with the idea of escaping again, and this time from the Marquis, she had found it an absorbing interest to be able to buy as many clothes as she wanted.

Also, it had been exciting to talk to the Marquis and to his friend Lord Hansketh.

She was actually never alone with her husband except after the dressmakers had fitted her with the gowns which he had ordered, when she went downstairs to show them to him when he was writing letters at his desk in the Study.

When he was not out of the house he always seemed to have a great deal of writing to do.

Cara gradually realised that he played an important part in the debates and business of the House of Lords, as well as being constantly in attendance upon the King.

His Majesty had recovered slowly from the inflammation of the lungs, and although he wished to attend his father's Funeral, his Physicians strongly urged him not to take the risk of doing so.

The King gave way to their entreaties and remained indoors, but he insisted on the Marquis being with him.

Now that he was no longer physically ill, he was exceedingly worried about his wife and in fact could speak of nothing else, and the Marquis was regaled with every incident of the Queen's behaviour in Europe.

He was also forced to read the long statements that the King was compiling in the hope that he might be able, sooner or later, to divorce her.

The whole story was so sordid that every time he came home the Marquis began to think that Cara at any rate was very different from what he had feared.

As he had realised when he first met her, she was quick-witted and had a gift of repartee that Henry Hansketh at any rate found very amusing.

"One thing about your wife, Ivo," he said to the Marquis in private, "is that she will never bore you as so many of your lady-loves have managed to do."

"Why should you say that?" the Marquis asked somewhat truculently.

"She has an original mind and a most unusual way of saying what she thinks," Lord Hansketh replied. "There are very few women like that, especially when they are young."

The Marquis had to admit this was true, but he was still resenting the manner in which he had been blackmailed into marriage by the Earl, and he still felt infuriated that Cara had shackled him.

At the same time, he had to admit that in the evenings when he, Henry, and his wife dined *a trois,* she contributed intelligently to the conversation and was also a good listener.

To Cara it was an experience she had never had before, which, although she did not admit it to herself, was sweeping away her fear of the male sex.

Because the Court was in mourning, no parties were being given, and the Marquis had said it would be a mistake for her to start to meet his friends until he could present her to them formally and make it, as he expressed it, a "grand occasion."

She knew this meant that she had to look right, and he wanted to show that there was nothing strange about their marriage, which had just been kept quiet until the King was well enough to be present.

"At the same time," she told herself, "I expect he is ashamed of me really, because I am not in the least the sort of wife he would have married if he had had the choice."

Just as Mrs. Peel had spoken about the Marquis almost as if he were a god, the Housekeeper and the rest of the servants at Broome House in Park Lane did the same.

Most of them had known him ever since he was a boy, and his successes first at Oxford, then in the Army, lost nothing in the telling.

They were ready to show Cara momentoes of every stage in his growing up, and because they believed her to be deeply in love with him, they assumed she would find every momento and anecdote about the man they admired something she would treasure and remember.

In the face of such adoration it was impossible to appear indifferent to what they wished to tell her, and she thought it would not only be ungracious to do so but also unkind.

She therefore found herself beginning to look at the Marquis in a very different light from the way she had before.

It was his secretary, Mr. Curtis, who told her of his importance in the political world and how the Prime Minister and Members of the Cabinet consulted him.

"Do they ever come here?" Cara asked, thinking she would like to see the Prime Minister and also the good-looking Lord Castlereagh, who was Secretary of State for Foreign Affairs.

"Sometimes they do," Mr. Curtis replied, "but usually they meet at Lord Harrowby's house in Grosvenor Square."

"I know that house!" Cara exclaimed. "It is next

door to my uncle's. He lives at Number Forty-three; and Lord Harrowby lives at Number Forty-four."

"That is right," Mr. Curtis said. "When the Cabinet was dining at Lord Harrowby's house on June 21, 1815, the Duke of Wellington's *Aide-de-Camp*, Major the Honourable Henry Percy, burst into the Dining-Room with the story of the victory of Waterloo and brought the Duke's despatch to Lord Bathurst, who was then Secretary of State for War."

"How exciting!" Cara exclaimed. "I wish I had been there!"

"I am afraid those dinner-parties do not include ladies," Mr. Curtis said with a smile.

"I think it is unfair that men have all the fun," Cara complained, and Mr. Curtis laughed.

She wished that when she was living with her uncle she had known of the exciting parties that were taking place next door, and she said now to Emily:

"Has Lord Harrowby, who lives next door to my uncle, had many guests lately?"

"I don't rightly know, M'Lady," Emily answered, "but I can soon find out."

"How can you do that?" Cara asked, and Emily looked coy.

"Well, as it happens, M'Lady, one of His Lordship's footmen has been courting me, so to speak. He makes all sorts of excuses to come round and see me. He's something of a chatter-box, and I expect he'll tell me anything I want to know."

Cara thought perhaps she should not ask outright for such information, and changing the subject she said:

"Has my uncle had any parties since I left?"

"Not big ones, M'Lady," Emily answered, "but there's a very strange man as comes to the house who Tim tells us has been in prison for abusing Lord Sidmouth."

Cara had heard the Marquis and Lord Hansketh

speaking of Lord Sidmouth and knew he was the Home Secretary.

"Why should my uncle want to have anything to do with a man who has been in prison?" she asked.

"His name's Thistlewood," Emily said, "and Tim says he's a nasty customer."

"What does he mean by that?" Cara questioned.

"I don't know, I don't listen to what Tim says. He's always saying things to make our flesh creep. But do you remember Albert? He was saying last night that this Mr. Thistlewood and the master are planning something, and he wouldn't be a bit surprised if it didn't include murder!"

Emily lowered her voice as she spoke to make what she was saying sound creepy.

"You cannot mean that," Cara said lightly.

Then she remembered that she had suspected her uncle of murdering her father, and if he could commit such a crime once, there was no reason why he should not do the same again.

She put the gown she was holding back in the wardrobe and said:

"I expect Albert is exaggerating, but tell me what he heard."

As she spoke, she knew that Albert must have been listening at the door of the room in which her uncle had been talking to this man Thistlewood.

"I thinks Albert talks a lot of nonsense!" Emily said. "I don't listen to half of what he says, but by the time I next comes to see you, M'Lady, I'll have got the whole story out of him."

After Emily had left, Cara thought over what she had said and decided it was unlikely that her uncle would involve himself in any activities which might be proved criminal.

At the same time, servants usually were surprisingly well informed about what was going on.

She was especially interested in Lord Harrowby's parties because she knew the Marquis attended them.

Because of the way he had talked to his friend Henry in front of her, she had begun to grow more and more interested in politics. She knew they were both deeply concerned that unless something was done there would be a social revolution with an attempt to overthrow the Government.

Often, she thought, they forgot that she was present and talked so seriously and so interestingly that she wished she could note down everything they said so that she would not forget it.

"I must find out about this man Thistlewood," she decided. "Perhaps he is the sort of person they fear may stir up trouble."

That evening the Marquis came back very late from the Palace, where the King had kept him while he railed furiously against the caricatures and satirical pamphlets that were appearing in the shops and were sold in the streets.

George Cruikshank, William Home, and a host of other satirists and artists championed the Queen and ridiculed the King.

In fact, there was only one print-seller who ventured to purvey Loyalist prints.

"Something must be done!" the King cried frantically, but the Marquis had no ready solution to the problem.

Every day produced dozens more aggressive and vulgar libels against the Monarch which were hawked in all the streets, and it was useless to make any attempt to check it.

"They must be aware that this will encourage the Queen to behave even worse than she is already!" the King said bitterly, and the Marquis could only feel desperately sorry for him.

It was quite a relief, after hours of talking about the

Queen and going over her misdeeds for the thousandth time, to find Cara waiting for him in the Drawing-Room.

She was looking very young and, as the Marquis admitted to himself, exceedingly lovely in one of the new gowns he had bought her.

It matched her eyes, as a number of others did, simply because the Marquis had found that one particular shade of pale green made her skin seem dazzlingly white and brought out the lights in her hair and in her eyes.

It also, he thought, gave her a somewhat elfish appearance which was unlike anything he had ever noticed in any of the women with whom he had been involved and which, although he still did not admit it, he found attractive.

Cara jumped to her feet as he entered the room.

"You are very late!" she said. "I wondered if something had happened to you."

"His Majesty kept me, and it is such a usual experience that I am almost tired of apologising."

"There is no need for you to do so," Cara replied. "Just as I accept it, so does the Chef, and I am sure that dinner will not be spoilt."

"It will not take me long to change," the Marquis answered, and hurried upstairs to his bedroom.

By the time he came downstairs again, Henry, who had been told that dinner would be later than usual, had arrived and was talking to Cara.

They were sitting together on the sofa, and the Marquis thought they were talking somewhat intimately as he came into the Drawing-Room.

It flashed through his mind that Henry, who had said that he admired both Cara's looks and her intelligence, might be making love to his wife.

Then he knew that the idea was not only disloyal but an impossibility.

However, during dinner the thought occurred again and again and began to irritate him.

"I was asking Lord Hansketh before dinner," Cara said as dessert was put on the table, "if he had ever heard of a man called Thistlewood."

"Her Ladyship suspects him of being a bad character who has been in prison," Lord Hansketh said.

"I have heard of him, and I have no idea why Cara should be interested in such a person," the Marquis said coldly.

He noticed that both Cara and Henry looked at him curiously, and he went on:

"Thistlewood is a renegade gentleman who gambled away all his money, then made a nuisance of himself by importuning Members of Parliament."

"I understood he went to prison for twelve months for abusing Lord Sidmouth," Cara said.

"I suppose you read about it in the newspapers," the Marquis replied. "He has certainly behaved abominably, and Sidmouth was quite right in taking a strong hand with such a trouble-maker."

"He is out of prison now," Cara insisted.

"If he is, and if he continues to make a nuisance of himself, he will soon be back there," the Marquis said.

"He might make a lot of trouble in the meantime," Henry remarked.

"I think it unlikely," the Marquis said crushingly, then changed the subject.

When Cara went to bed, she thought over what had been said and was sure that the Marquis, if he became aware that Thistlewood was seeing her uncle, would suspect that they were plotting something unpleasant.

For all she had heard from the conversations between the Marquis and Lord Hansketh, it seemed certain that the revolution they both feared would not take place until those who wanted to rebel had the right sort of leader.

She was imaginative enough to realise that what the Marquis had called a "renegade gentleman" would be just the sort of person to organise a rebellion and give it direction and purpose.

'I must find out more from Emily,' she thought.

As Henry was leaving he had asked:

"Are you riding in the Park tomorrow morning, Ivo?"

"Of course," the Marquis replied with a smile.

"Then I will meet you there," Henry said. "I bought a new horse yesterday, and before I send it down to my place in the country I want you to have a look at him."

"I would like that," the Marquis answered, "and as soon as I can get His Majesty's permission, I intend to take Cara to Broome, and I hope you will accompany us there."

"You know I never refuse one of your invitations," Henry said, "nor the opportunity to ride your horses."

"As it happens, I am looking forward to riding one of my own," the Marquis said. "You have not yet seen *Agamemnon*."

"That is an animal I am very eager to meet," Henry said with a smile, "after all you have told me about him."

Cara listened with interest.

She was aware by now how much his horses meant to the Marquis, and she noticed that when he talked about them there was a very different note in his voice from when he talked about anything else.

"Perhaps he should have married a horse!" she told herself with a little smile, and wondered if he would ever love a woman as much as she was certain he loved *Agamemnon*.

She knew that it irked him to have to be in London for so long, and the only compensation was that he rode very early in the Park, when he had the place almost to himself.

'When my riding-habit is ready,' she thought, 'I will ask if I can accompany him.'

She had the uncomfortable feeling that he would think her superfluous to his enjoyment and would prefer her to continue as she was doing now, driving with a groom later in the day to get the air and not taking any really active exercise.

'When we go to Broome,' she thought, 'perhaps I will be able to demonstrate to him how well I can ride.'

Because they had been estranged from the very moment of their marriage, she found it difficult to ask for special favours which concerned her own enjoyment.

She still vaguely thought of the idea of leaving the Marquis, and she asked Emily to bring her another suit from the attic in Grosvenor Square.

"What've you done with the one you ran away in, M'Lady?" Emily asked.

"The Housekeeper at Broome looked at it with horror, then doubtless burnt it!" Cara replied.

Emily laughed.

"I always thought 'twas very brave of you, M'Lady, going off on your own like that, not that I blamed you, with His Lordship beating you like a dog and saying as how you had to marry that horrible gentleman."

"I shall always be very grateful to you for telling me about him," Cara said. "If you had not done so, I might have been married to him by now!"

She shivered as she thought of it, and told herself that although she might dislike being married to any man, at least the Marquis did not beat her.

Although automatically she had locked the communicating door between his room and hers and the door into the passage at night, ever since the first evening when he had said he wanted to talk to her, she knew he had never again made any effort to come to her.

When on that first night he had knocked on her door, she had been frightened.

It had seemed impossible, when he had been forced into marriage by her uncle in such a barbarous manner, that the Marquis should think of her as a woman.

And yet she could not be sure.

Because of what she felt about her uncle, Sir

Mortimer, and in fact all men, she had been terrified that the Marquis might try to touch her.

Now that she knew him better, she was certain that he was not in the slightest degree interested in her as a woman and was in fact concerned only that she should not shame him while she bore his name.

She had gradually began to relax; her heart no longer jumped with fear when he came into the room, nor did she watch him apprehensively as if he were a wild aminal who might pounce on her at any moment.

Just as the scars were beginning to fade from her back, and by now could barely be seen, so her mind was adjusting itself to living with the Marquis in comparative friendliness.

The next morning she heard him leave his bedroom at seven-thirty and knew he would be going riding in the Park.

For the first time she had a sudden urge to go with him and be with him, and she decided that when he returned she would definitely ask if she too could ride when the Park was empty.

Then it crossed her mind that perhaps, although she was unaware of it, he went to meet somebody he found attractive and who had ridden with him in the past before they were married.

The servants had not omitted to relate to her amongst their other memories what a success the Marquis was with the famous Beauties of the *Beau Monde*.

"I thought at one time His Lordship might marry the daughter of the Duke of Newcastle," the House-keeper had said. "A lovelier young lady you never saw, and she would certainly have looked her best wearing the Broome diamonds at the Opening of Parliament and at the Balls given at Carlton House."

"Oh, I never believed she'd a chance!" Robinson had replied, who was still maiding Cara.

"Who did you fancy then, may I ask, Miss Robin-son?" the Housekeeper had enquired.

"There were plenty to choose from," Robinson replied, "but I always thought the loveliest lady of them all was Lady Aileen Wynter, and there's no doubt she laid her heart at His Lordship's feet."

"Let me think—oh, I remembers her now, and very sad for her it was when her husband was killed in Spain."

"She forgot about him when she met His Lordship," Robinson said with a smirk.

Then, feeling that they were being too indiscreet in front of Cara, they had hurriedly gone back to tales about the Marquis when he was a small boy.

Because he was so handsome, Cara thought, there were bound to have been numerous women in his life, and yet he had not wished to marry any of them, but had wanted to remain single and independent as she had wanted to do.

"If I run away, he will never find me and he will be free," she told herself.

Then she realised that she was back at the same place where her fantasies always began and ended, seeking freedom but unable to know how she could get it.

* * *

"Here you are, M'Lady, and I think it'll fit you as well as the other one did," Emily said.

She had arrived late in the afternoon when Cara had come back from a drive in the Park.

As she spoke, Emily opened a rather untidy parcel and produced another suit consisting of trousers and a coat which Cara thought must have belonged to her father when he was a boy.

"It is rather bigger than the last one," she said, "and the trousers are too long."

"You can turn 'em up at the bottom," Emily said, "or I'll stitch 'em up for Your Ladyship."

"I will not bother now," Cara replied. "But I will hide it away so that it is here if I want it."

"I can't think that you should want it, M'Lady," Emily said. "You don't want to run away from His Lordship! He's a fine man! His Royal Highness thinks the world of him."

Cara had been told this before, and she asked:

"Have you anything more to tell me about Mr. Thistlewood?"

"I were just going to tell you about him, M'Lady," Emily answered. "Albert says there's ever such strange things going on, and he thinks Lord Harrowby himself is in danger."

"Why should he think that?" Cara enquired.

"Mr. Thistlewood told His Lordship that if they could dispose of Lord Harrowby and the Members of the Cabinet, then they'll be able to make the mob who're fed up with the whole Government march on all the important buildings, starting with the Barracks in Hyde Park."

Cara stared at Emily incredulously.

"What are you saying, Emily?" she asked. "Start at the beginning and tell me exactly what Albert overheard."

Because she had spoken sharply, she thought Emily might be frightened and refuse to talk. So she added quickly:

"We both know that Albert listens at the door, and I am not saying I disapprove, because I am sure my uncle and Mr. Thistlewood are up to no good, and it is important for us to know what they are concocting."

"Yes, of course, M'Lady, but you knows what Albert's like when he tells a story. Half of it may be true and the other half false."

"Yes, I know that," Cara agreed, "but tell me what he said anyway."

"This Mr. Thistlewood, from all I hears," Emily began, "has a whole band of people as follows him, and Albert thinks they're planning when Lord Harrowby next gives a dinner-party to break into Number Forty-four and murder them all!"

"I do not believe it!" Cara exclaimed incredulously.

"That's what he told the master. They've got it all planned out."

Cara was silent for a moment. Then she said:

"Where does Mr. Thistlewood live?"

"Albert doesn't know that," Emily said. "He meets those he leads in a stable-yard in Cato Street."

"Where is that?" Cara enquired.

"Somewhere off the Edgware Road, and Albert heard them say they've all sorts of weapons there, and their revolution when it does start'll be a big one!"

Cara shivered.

It was, she felt, just the sort of intrigue her uncle would enjoy.

However, it seemed impossible to believe that he would really plot with Revolutionaries to overthrow the Government or even to make trouble.

She had read in the newspapers what was happening in the North.

She knew that last year at St. Peter's Field, which had been almost like a battlefield, fifty thousand unarmed cotton operatives had been fired on by the Yeomanry.

There had been a great deal of anger about it, and yet, Members of the Government were still asking for stronger and more repressive measures against any form of rebellion or protest.

"I'll find out more from Albert," Emily was saying. She obviously enjoyed supplying Cara with the information she had asked for.

"Yes, do that," Cara said. "How often do these men meet Mr. Thistlewood?"

"I think every night, M'Lady. Albert said he heard the master say this morning in the Library:

"'You tell them what I've said, Thistlewood, and report to me tomorrow morning.'"

Cara said nothing more and Emily hurried away.
Not long afterwards, Robinson came to her room to help
her change for dinner.

She put on one of the beautiful gowns that had been
made for her in Bond Street, and thought as she looked
at herself in the mirror that the Marquis would be
pleased that this one in particular would be exactly as he
wished it to be.

It was white, trimmed with small bunches of mag-
nolias with their very dark green leaves, and it made the
gown very striking and quite different from any gown
Cara had ever seen before.

She thought it must be unusual for a man to know so
much about dresses. Then she suddenly realised why he
was such an expert in this field as in others.

It had never struck her until this moment that she
was not the first woman for whom he had chosen clothes.

She did not know why, but she suddenly felt
dissatisfied with her own appearance and petulantly
turned away from the mirror.

Then she glanced at the clock and realised it was
later than she had thought.

"I must hurry," she said to Robinson. "His Lordship
will be annoyed if I'm late and spoil the dinner."

"I don't think His Lordship's back yet, M'Lady,"
Robinson replied.

"Not back? But it is nearly quarter-to-eight!"

Without saying any more, Cara opened her bedroom door and ran downstairs.

Bateson, the Butler, was in the Hall.

"Is His Lordship back?" she asked.

"I was just about to send upstairs to tell Your
Ladyship that His Lordship has sent a message with the
carriage," the Butler replied, "to inform Your Ladyship
that he deeply regrets he cannot return home for dinner
as His Majesty requires him."

For a moment Cara did not answer. Then in a voice
that sounded a little flat she said:

"Please tell the Chef I am ready for dinner."

"Very good, M'Lady."

* * *

The Marquis, driving back to his house, was thinking not of his wife, who had had to dine alone without him, but of the King and his problems.

Of these, however, he was heartily sick, and he had already informed the Lord Chamberlain that he intended to leave for Broome the day after tomorrow.

"I must get away," he said, "and the sooner the better."

Then, as if he felt he must explain, he added:

"I have promised to dine with Harrowby and the Cabinet tomorrow, but that is the last engagement I intend to have in London for at least a week, or perhaps two."

"I cannot blame you," the Lord Chamberlain replied. "With the late King's death and His Majesty's illness, you have not yet had a honeymoon."

"That is true!" the Marquis exclaimed, but he did not elaborate on the matter.

Now as he neared Broome House he thought it might be a good idea for him to get to know Cara better when they were in the country.

He was already aware that she was a good rider, and he thought it would interest her to try out some of his horses, not those which were as wild as *Agamemnon* but which needed a strong hand.

'It is certainly an interest we have in common,' he thought.

He found himself thinking how attractive she had looked the previous evening in one of the gowns he had practically designed himself, and in which he realised, once social festivities recommenced, she would stand out.

The carriage drew up outside his house and the footman ran to open the door.

The Marquis stepped out, and as he walked into the Hall, Bateson said:

"Excuse me, M'Lord, but a young woman, a woman called Emily, insists on seeing Your Lordship. I told her it was too late, but she waited and asked me to tell you that it's a question of life and death!"

Bateson spoke with the supercilious manner of a servant who relays a message in which he does not believe.

For a moment the Marquis wondered where he had heard the name "Emily" before, then remembered how Cara had told him it was Emily who had helped her to escape from her uncle's house.

"I will see the young woman in the Study," he said.

He walked into the room in which he worked, and wondered what he was about to hear and why Emily had not first discussed with Cara what she had to say.

He glanced at the clock, and seeing that it was nearly midnight, he thought that Cara would be asleep and that was why, quite rightly, Bateson had not disturbed her.

The door opened and Bateson said in a very disapproving voice:

"The young woman to see you, M'Lord!"

His first glance at Emily told the Marquis that she was a respectable-looking girl, neatly dressed in black and wearing a black bonnet trimmed with ribbons that tied under her chin and with a heavy woollen shawl over her shoulders.

She curtseyed and stood just inside the door, waiting for him to speak to her.

"Good-evening!" the Marquis said. "I understand your name is Emily and you are a housemaid Her Ladyship knew when she lived in Grosvenor Square."

"That's right, M'Lord, and I had to see Your Lordship—I had to reelly!"

"Is something wrong?" the Marquis enquired.

"Very, very wrong, M'Lord, and it's my fault. But I

swear I never imagined Her Ladyship would do anything so foolish when she asked me to get her another suit of clothes. I just thought she was planning some sort of escapade. But nothing like this, I swear it, M'Lord!"

The agitated way in which Emily spoke made the Marquis stare at her in surprise.

Then he sat down at his desk, indicating an upright chair at the other side of it.

"Suppose you sit down, Emily," he said, "and tell me what all this is about. At the moment, I cannot understand what you are saying."

Emily crossed the room to the chair almost as if her legs would barely carry her there. Then she sat down, clasping her hands together in an agitated manner.

"When Tim tells me he'd seen Her Ladyship, I didn't believe it!" she said.

"Who is Tim?" the Marquis interrupted.

"He's the scullery-boy, M'Lord. He's always snooping and prying about, and it's him as told the master that Her Ladyship climbed into your carriage when she ran away."

"I understand," the Marquis said. "And what has he seen now?"

"He sees Her Ladyship going into that place where all them murderers hang out. When I tells her about it, I'd no idea she'd do such a thing! If they finds her, they'll kill her, M'Lord!"

The Marquis looked bewildered.

"What murderers? And how do you know where Her Ladyship has gone?"

"Tim seen her, M'Lord! Seen her not two hours ago, and when he comes back and tells me, I could hardly believe my ears!"

"Where did he see her?" the Marquis asked.

His voice was calm.

He had known when he interrogated men during the war that it was the greatest mistake to shout or hurry them, because then they became completely inarticulate.

"It's the place in Cato Street, M'Lord," Emily replied, "where them Revolutionaries meet as is led by Mr. Thistlewood!"

The Marquis stiffened.

"Did you say Thistlewood?" he enquired.

"Yes, M'Lord. He's the man as has been coming to the house to talk to the master, and Albert—that's the footman—overheard what they said."

"What did they say?"

"They're planning, M'Lord, at the next dinner-party to be given at Number Forty-four, to murder Lord Harrowby and all his guests."

For a moment the Marquis was too surprised to speak. Then he said:

"And you told Her Ladyship about this?"

"Yes, M'Lord, but I never realised—I never thought she'd do anything about it or visit them murderers herself."

"And you tell me this is what she has done now?"

"Yes, M'Lord. Tim sees her. Sees her dressed in the suit I brought here from the attics, going into the stable just before Mr. Thistlewood and them as follows him arrives."

The Marquis's lips tightened and he said, still in his calm voice:

"Did Tim tell you how many men there were?"

"Two dozen or so, M'Lord, perhaps more."

"And you say this place is in Cato Street?"

"Yes, M'Lord, and Tim says if they find Her Ladyship, they'll kill her for sure!"

"Then let us hope they do not do so," the Marquis said. "Thank you, Emily, for being brave enough to come and tell me what is happening."

"I had to, M'Lord. I had to! Even if it loses me my job, I couldn't let Her Ladyship be killed or hurt by them thugs, could I?"

"No, of course not," the Marquis agreed.

He looked at Emily, then he said:

"What I am going to suggest, Emily, is that you do not go back to Grosvenor Square, where you might be in danger for bringing me this information. Instead I suggest you stay here. My Housekeeper will find you a bed, and tomorrow we will discuss what can be done about you in the future."

Tears ran down Emily's cheeks.

"Thank you, M'Lord, thank you!" she said. "I was sure they'd think it strange when I runs out of the house after what Tim told me. They knows I love Her Ladyship an' would never let anything happen to her."

"Nothing will, and you will be safe here," the Marquis said.

He rose to his feet and strode from the Study into the Hall. While he was giving his orders sharply to Bateson, he was wondering if and how he would be able to save Cara.

Chapter Seven

Driving towards Cato Street in the closed Brougham that he sometimes used in London, the Marquis could hardly believe that what Emily had told him was true.

Now he remembered saying to Cara:

"I am dining in tonight, but not tomorrow, as I have to meet the Cabinet at Lord Harrowby's."

She had made no comment at the time, and he had not thought that to be significant.

But now he was sure that the reason she had gone to Cato Street was to find out if Emily's story was true and they really intended to murder the Cabinet at Lord Harrowby's house the next evening.

It seemed incredible, and yet, as the Marquis had said so often, the seeds of revolution had been growing steadily and nobody had done anything about it.

To make certain that Cara was actually out and not asleep in bed, when he had gone upstairs to change from his evening-clothes he had opened the door of her bedroom.

If it had been locked as it had been every night since she had married him, he would have known that his fears were unnecessary.

But when the door opened, even before he could see by the light in the passage that the bed was empty and unslept in, he knew that Cara had impulsively done the most crazy thing in her whole life.

The Marquis did not underestimate the danger she was in, and after he told his coachman to wait in a quiet square off the Edgware Road, he walked alone towards Cato Street, keeping in the shadows.

As by now it was after midnight, everything was very quiet and there was very little traffic.

There was not even the usual number of unsavoury characters looking in the gutter for scraps or anything they could beg or steal from some gentleman returning home after imbibing too freely.

Anyway, the Edgware Road was not a place for drunken Bucks, and when the Marquis did see somebody in the distance, he kept out of sight in case he should get involved in anything unpleasant.

He found Cato Street quite easily, having a good idea of where it was situated.

It was a small, insignificant street with a few dilapidated stables facing some squalid houses that were badly in need of repair.

Some of these were empty, but there was a Tavern, its windows throwing a golden light onto the cobbled road and illuminating a stable opposite, which the Marquis, more by instinct than anything else, felt must be the place Emily had described to him.

The door, which was broken at the hinges, was ajar; but he did not go near it. Instead he waited in the shadow of a doorway on the other side of the road.

After a minute or so he realised that the house against which he was standing was empty, the windows were broken, and the door itself was ajar.

He therefore let himself in, being careful to avoid a creaking and broken board, then stood watching the stable opposite.

He thought a flicker of light came from within the building, but he could not be sure.

Everything seemed very quiet and, as such, menacing.

It was then that he began to be desperately afraid for Cara.

"How could she possibly," he asked himself, "do anything so rash as to go alone dressed as a boy and listen to the plots and plans of men who will think nothing of murdering anybody who might betray them?"

He had to admit that she certainly had tremendous courage, and he could not imagine that any other woman of his acquaintance would take such risks.

Yet, ever since he had known Cara she had been unpredictable.

She was so small, delicately made, and lovely that he could not bear to think of her being handled roughly and perhaps tortured to tell what she knew before she was killed.

For the first time since he had left home, he thought that perhaps he should have brought help with him.

Yet, if Emily was right and there were twenty-four men plotting in the stable opposite, he would have required at least an equal number to face them, and where could he have got so many at this time of night?

Then as he began to think that waiting to see what would happen was intolerable and he would have to take some course of action, slowly and quietly the broken door of the stable was pulled open.

The Marquis held his breath, then saw a man peep out to look up and down the street.

Obviously reassured to see that there was nobody about, he opened the door a little wider and they came trooping out.

They were exactly the type of men that the Marquis had expected to be engaged in such a plot.

They were not humble labourers who had every reason to protest against hunger and unemployment, but malcontents of a higher class who were always prepared in any argument to use brute force rather than words.

There were large men and small, all with the stamp of rebels on them, the Marquis thought, and also the look of buccaneers who were prepared to risk life and limb if the plunder was worthwhile.

They emerged in absolute silence, which made it more sinister than if they were talking with one another.

Then they hurried away, separating in different directions as if they had been told not to keep in a group, until last of all came a man who the Marquis was sure was their leader—Thistlewood.

He was obviously a man of better birth and would pass as a gentleman.

At the same time, although it was hard to see his face clearly from across the road, the Marquis was sure he was a brutal and callous type who was thinking entirely of his own interests rather than of the men he was leading into trouble.

He pulled the stable door to behind him.

There was no lock, but the Marquis knew this was a positive recommendation, for any door bolted and barred in this sort of street would give an indication that there was something inside to steal, and the place would immediately be broken into.

When Thistlewood had shut the stable door as close as he could, he squared his shoulders, then hesitated and glanced at the Tavern as if he felt in need of a drink.

He took a few steps towards it, and in the light coming from the windows the Marquis could see him more clearly and knew that he was looking at a man who was born to be a criminal.

There was something cruel about the thin tightness of his lips, and the Marquis thought too that he looked elated, presumably at the result of the meeting, and there was an unmistakable stir of triumph about him.

Then he obviously changed his mind and walked

away down Cato Street in the direction of the Edgware Road.

The Marquis waited until he was out of sight. Then, stepping out of the house in which he had been hiding, he hurried to the stable.

He opened the door very quietly, knowing from his experience of war that men had often lost their lives when they thought the enemy had left a certain post, only to find that one had been left behind as a guard.

Only after he had waited for a second or two, having opened the door, did he step inside the stable.

It was dark and smelt of musty hay, and just in front of him he could see the loft in which the conspirators had met.

There was no sign of a ladder anywhere, but he thought that before he left Thistlewood would undoubtedly have hidden it in case it should be stolen.

The Marquis walked farther into the darkness, then stood still, listening.

There was only silence. Then very softly, making his voice little more than a whisper, he called:

"Cara!"

For a moment he thought he was mistaken and she was not there.

Then he heard a murmur of surprise and a moment later her voice asked:

"Is that . . . really . . . you?"

"I am here," he replied. "Where are you?"

"I . . . cannot get . . . down."

Because it was impossible to see anything in the direction from which her voice came, the Marquis pulled the door open a little farther, then walked deep into the stable, where he stopped to ask again:

"Where are you?"

"I am . . . here," she replied, and her voice came from above his head.

He realised then that she had climbed over a

broken manger and up into the hay-rack above it so that she was just below the floor of the loft above her.

He walked to stand immediately below her and put up his arms.

"I will not let you fall."

She put one leg over the side of the hay-rack and leant over, her arms going out towards him to hold on to his shoulders.

"You are quite safe," he said. "Let yourself go."

She did as he told her and fell into his arms.

He had braced himself for the impact, then he was holding her tightly against him, and as he did so he felt her arms go round his neck, and she said in a terrified whisper:

"They are . . . going to . . . kill you! Oh . . . Ivo, they are . . . going to . . . kill you . . . and everyone else . . . tomorrow night!"

He knew as she spoke how frightened she was, and he could feel her heart beating frantically against his.

His arms tightened and he looked down in the darkness to where he knew her face would be and said:

"How could you come here? How could you do anything so incredibly . . ."

He stopped.

Then as he knew he held her safe and there was no need for words, his lips found hers and he kissed her.

As he did so he knew that he was in love.

While he was waiting on the other side of the road he had been desperate with anxiety and fear, but now the relief of knowing that she was safe was sweeping over him with an irrepressible joy that could only be love.

He had never thought, never imagined for one moment, that he would fall in love with Cara, who was everything he disapproved of in a woman.

But now as his lips held hers captive he knew that, although he would have never admitted it even to himself, every day she had entwined herself closer and closer round his heart until he was in love as he had never thought it possible to be.

To Cara it was as if the Heavens opened and she found herself in a blaze of light instead of in a darkness in which there was only horror and fear.

Without even knowing she was doing so, she pressed herself closer to the Marquis and her lips responded to his.

How long they were held together by that kiss neither of them had any idea.

But at last the Marquis raised his head and felt as if he had come back to reality as he said:

"For God's sake, let us get out of this place! I was so afraid those devils would kill you."

"They . . . intend to . . . kill you," Cara murmured.

Yet, he knew by the way she spoke that for the moment the words meant nothing and she had been swept, as he had been, by the ecstasy of their kiss into the sky and it was difficult to come back to earth.

Still holding her in his arms, the Marquis walked towards the door.

Only when he reached it did he stop, as the first of the conspirators had done, to look up and down the street before he emerged.

There was nobody about and the place seemed quiet and deserted.

Then hurriedly, because he was still afraid for Cara, he carried her across the road and back the way he had come after leaving his carriage.

She did not speak, and he knew without being told that she was still caught in the rapture they had felt when their lips had touched, and it was hard to think of anything else.

Only when the carriage was in sight did she ask:

"Do you . . . want me to . . . walk?"

"Stay as you are," the Marquis said. "I am still desperately afraid of losing you."

His arms tightened as he spoke, and Cara felt that she had never known such safety or such happiness.

At the sight of them the footman jumped down from the box and opened the carriage door, and the Marquis laid Cara gently down on the back seat before he stepped in himself.

The footman put the fur-lined rug over their knees and asked:

"Home, M'Lord?"

"Yes, home," the Marquis replied.

Then, when the footman had shut the door and scrambled up on the box and the horses set off, the Marquis put his arm round Cara.

A question came to his mind that he was longing to ask her.

Then by the candle in the silver lantern fixed above the seat opposite them he saw her face tipped up to his, her eyes wide and excited as she looked at him enquiringly, and he knew that the only thing of importance was that he should kiss her.

As if he was still haunted by the dangers through which she had passed, he pulled her almost roughly against him, and once again his lips were on hers, kissing her fiercely and possessively because he was afraid he might have lost her.

As he did so, he knew that the feelings rising within him were different from anything he had ever felt in his life before.

He realised that they had been activated by fear, but he knew there was something else in this kiss that was different from any he had given or received before.

It was not only that he desired Cara as a woman and that her lips were soft, sweet, and very innocent beneath his.

There was also something intensely spiritual in his feelings, which told him, through an instinct which had never deceived him, that she was what he had been seeking all his life and never found.

He could not explain it, he knew only that it was there and that he loved her with an emotion which no other woman had ever aroused in him.

He wanted to protect her and at the same time to give her a happiness that came from something Divine within them both.

Only when they had driven quite a long way towards Berkeley Square did the Marquis raise his head, and Cara said in a rapt little tone he had never heard from her before:

"I . . . love you . . . oh, Ivo . . . I love you but I did not . . . know it until I . . . heard those wicked men . . . plotting to . . . k-kill you!"

At last the Marquis was able to say what he had wanted to say earlier.

"How could you do anything so crazy, so mad, as to go to that place alone? How could you have risked your life?"

"I had to be . . . certain that Albert was not making it up . . . that if . . . you went to . . . Lord Harrowby's dinner tomorrow . . . night you would . . . d-die."

Her voice broke on the last word, and the Marquis asked:

"Would that have worried you? I thought you wanted to be free of me."

"I love you, although I did not realise it," Cara replied. "But I . . . do, and . . . please . . . I want to . . . stay with . . . you."

For a moment the Marquis did not answer, and she said quickly:

"You are not . . . angry with . . . me?"

"I am not angry," the Marquis assured her, "you only frightened me as I have never been frightened before. Oh, my darling, do you swear to me that you will never do anything like this again?"

He felt Cara quiver at the endearment, then as if

her feelings were too much for her she hid her face
against his neck.

"If you . . . let me . . . stay with . . . you," she
whispered, "I will be safe . . . but I must be . . . sure
that you will be . . . safe too."

"I will be," the Marquis answered, "because, thanks
to you, Harrowby's dinner-party will not take place
tomorrow evening."

He felt Cara give a deep sigh of relief, but when he
would have turned her face up to his to kiss her again, he
was aware that they were back in Berkeley Square.

There was only a night-footman on duty in the Hall,
because the Marquis before leaving had deliberately told
Bateson to go to bed and not wait up for him.

He had known how Cara would be dressed and had
no wish for more servants than necessary to see her in
trousers.

"Go straight to your room, my precious," he said as
the carriage came to a standstill. "I will bring you
something to eat and drink. Then you can tell me what
happened."

From the light streaming through the Hall he saw
the smile she gave him, and he thought that, strangely
dressed though she might be, nobody could look more
beautiful.

As the footman opened the door of the carriage, she
slipped past him and was running up the stairs almost
before the man realised what had happened.

The Marquis took his time dismissing his coachman
and came into the house to hand over his tall hat and
cape to a flunkey.

Then, going to his Study to collect the bottle of
champagne which he knew would be there and a plate of
pâté sandwiches, he carried them up the stairs, thinking
as he did so that he felt happier than he had ever felt in
his whole life.

It was as if the curtain were rising on a Play he had
never seen before, but which he knew would be more

thrilling than anything he had ever dreamt of or encountered because Cara was waiting for him.

When his valet had helped him to undress and put on a long silk robe that reached the ground, holding the champagne and sandwiches in one hand, he opened the communicating door between his room and Cara's.

He knew that tonight it would not be locked.

As he went through it he saw her sitting up in bed, and he thought that in her transparent nightgown and with her gold curls glinting in the light from the candles, nobody could look more exquisitely feminine and excitingly desirable.

He put the champagne and the sandwiches down on a table.

Then, as if it was impossible for the moment to think about them, he sat down facing Cara on the side of the mattress to say in his deep voice:

"You are here! I have brought you back safely, and for the moment I can think of nothing else."

"I had to . . . go to . . . see if you . . . really were in . . . danger," Cara said, "and, oh, Ivo, now you must save all the . . . others because they . . . intend to kill them."

"You must tell me about it," the Marquis said vaguely.

But his eyes were on her face and the softness of her lips.

"I love you!" he said. "How could I not have known it before now? You must never in any circumstances ever risk your life again, because you belong to me."

"Do you . . . really love me?" Cara asked. "I cannot believe it."

"I will make you believe it," the Marquis said, "and, darling, I know now that what I am feeling for you is what I have always wanted, searched for, and longed for, although I was unaware of it."

Cara gave a little cry of happiness. Then she said:

"How can I have been so stupid as not to know the

moment I saw you that you were the man I dreamt might be . . . somewhere in the . . . world, and whom I could . . . love as Mama loved Papa?"

"And as I love you."

As he spoke he bent forward to put his arms round her.

As her head fell back against the pillow, he looked down at her for a long moment, as if he must engrave her beauty on his heart forever before his lips found hers.

Then he was kissing her with a long, slow, passionate kiss which was more ecstatic, more marvellous than their kiss had been before, until Cara's arms went round his neck to draw him closer, and still closer. . . .

* * *

A long time later, Cara stirred against the Marquis's shoulder to ask:

"How could I have been so . . . foolish as to waste so much time in thinking I . . . must leave you, when I know now that if I had done so . . . all I would want to do would be to . . . die?"

"You are not going to die, my beloved," the Marquis answered. "You are going to live with me, belong to me, and, as I told you once before, I will kill anybody who attempts to take you from me."

"No one will be able to do that," Cara said. "But I did not . . . know that love was so . . . wonderful and so overwhelming."

"I did not frighten you?" the Marquis asked.

"How could I be frightened when I adore and worship you?"

"You were frightened of me the first night you came here," the Marquis said, "and it has worried me ever since."

"I will never be frightened *of* you again, only *for* you, in case that horrible man Thistlewood or Uncle Lionel should hurt you."

As if her words brought back the agonies they had both been through, the Marquis pulled her even closer to him, and his lips were on her forehead as he said:

"I suppose, my adorable one, you will have to tell me what happened tonight, but for the moment I can think of nothing but you and the happiness you have given me."

"It is . . . so . . . wonderful that you . . . love me," Cara said, "but you will have to save Lord Harrowby and the Cabinet."

"I will do that," the Marquis said, "but first, tell me again that you love me and that I am not dreaming this whole situation."

Cara gave a little chuckle of delight.

"It does seem incredible, does it not?" she agreed. "I made Emily bring me another suit because I was vaguely thinking I must run away from you. Then tonight, when she told me that Uncle Lionel was plotting with that man Thistlewood to kill everybody who goes to the dinner with Lord Harrowby tomorrow night . . . I knew I had to . . . save you."

"You could have warned me about it without taking such risks," the Marquis said.

"I did not think you would believe me," Cara answered, "and I felt as if Fate was driving me to go find out for myself. Only when I was listening to the evil things they were planning did I know how much I . . . loved you and that even if they . . . killed me I had to save you."

Her words made the Marquis hold her closer still. Then he kissed her cheeks and was seeking her mouth before he said:

"Tell me the whole story. Then we can think only about ourselves and forget the conspirators at least until tomorrow morning."

Cara put her hand across his chest as if she would protect him.

"I found my way to Cato Street because Emily had

said the men met there in a stable, and I looked at all the stables before I found the right one."

"How did you know which one it was?" the Marquis enquired.

"The others either had horses in them, or the lofts had collapsed completely from neglect and it would be impossible for anyone to sit in them."

"Go on," the Marquis prompted. "Having found the stable, what did you do then?"

"I realised that if I was discovered I would be in terrible trouble," Cara said, "but as the door was open, I saw the broken manger and rack above it, and I knew that if I could climb into it, no one entering through the door was likely to see me. Also, as my head would be against the floor of the loft, I would be able to hear what was said."

"That was clever of you," the Marquis said, "but still dangerous."

"I only had to wait for about fifteen minutes," Cara went on, "before the first man appeared. He set up the ladder, which had been hidden, fortunately at the other end of the stable, and climbed into the loft. Then they all began arriving, one after another, and they sat talking amongst themselves until Mr. Thistlewood came."

"How did you know it was him?" the Marquis enquired.

"Because they spoke very respectfully to him when they said 'good-evening.' He told them he had seen Uncle Lionel, who had insisted that the first person they . . . murdered was to be . . . you!"

There was so much horror in Cara's voice that the Marquis held her even closer against him and felt her heart beating against his.

"It is all over now, my precious," he said softly, "but you have to tell me what else occurred."

"Mr. Thistlewood went through the whole plan and they decided that one of their number should call at Lord Harrowby's house while dinner was in progress, and he would pretend he was a messenger with a special despatch."

The Marquis listened intently as Cara continued:

"While he spoke to the footman, the rest of the conspirators, who would be hidden in small groups in the Square, would be watching."

Her fingers tightened on the Marquis's bare shoulder as she said:

"Oh, Ivo, they have planned to murder the entire Cabinet, including the servants if they resist, and a man called Ings, who is a Butcher, said he intended to cut off the heads of Lord Castlereagh and Lord Sidmouth!"

The Marquis drew in his breath incredulously, but he did not interrupt, and Cara went on:

"He had two bags for them, and he said he also wanted the right hand of Lord Castlereagh, which he felt would be a valuable souvenir!"

"They must all be mad!" the Marquis ejaculated.

"They sounded mad," Cara agreed, "and when they have killed everybody they plan to fire a rocket from the house as a signal to their friends."

"What will happen then?"

"An oil-shop, which they said was near Grosvenor Square, is to be set on fire to gather the crowds."

"Did they really say that?" the Marquis enquired. "What was the idea?"

"Mr. Thistlewood said the fire would collect a huge mob which would become wild with excitement at the sight of the mangled remains of the Cabinet. They would then be able to capture the Barracks in Hyde Park."

"I have never heard such a crazy scheme in the whole of my life!" the Marquis exclaimed.

"That is not all. Thistlewood said that if they take hundreds of rioters with them, they will sack the Bank of England, occupy the Tower of London, and throw open the gates of Newgate Prison."

"Such a plan seems absolutely incredible!" the

Marquis said. "And you really think your uncle is aware of this?"

"Mr. Thistlewood spoke of him proudly," Cara answered, "and I am sure it was Uncle Lionel who told them that they will be able to establish a Provisional Government and proclaim it on the steps of the Mansion House."

The Marquis remembered the Earl boasting that he had him at his mercy. Now he knew that the tables were turned: the Earl was at his mercy and would be hanged as a traitor.

However, he did not say so to Cara, but merely asked:

"What else did they say?"

"They checked the number of guns, pikes, and hand grenades they had, and Mr. Thistlewood arranged for them to collect all these before they go to their hiding-places in the Square tomorrow night. He also said that Uncle Lionel had given him a large sum of money to buy more weapons, especially pistols."

The Marquis was sure the Earl imagined that the gratitude of the conspirators would ensure him a high place in the new Government and that he would be able to make a considerable amount of money out of the revolution.

"What happened then?" he asked Cara.

"They all swore their allegiance to Mr. Thistlewood and said they would follow him faithfully and place him in the seat of power as Governor of the country, once everybody in the present Government was dead."

The Marquis could hardly believe that what he was hearing was the truth.

Yet, if the conspirators did not manage to achieve all their ambitions, they could certainly do a great deal of harm, and twenty-four of them without any difficulty would be able to murder all those who were present at Lord Harrowby's for dinner tomorrow.

"It was very brave and wonderful of you, my

darling," he said gently, "to find out what you have, and I know how grateful the Prime Minister and especially Lord Harrowby will be when tomorrow night the rebels are arrested and imprisoned. At the same time, I cannot have you involved."

Cara looked up at him, and he explained:

"As my wife and the Marchioness of Broome, it would cause a great deal of undesirable gossip if it were known that you had listened to the eavesdropping of a servant, and disguised as a boy had overheard the plans of cut-throats and Revolutionaries."

"I understand."

"I shall therefore tell only the Prime Minister how I obtained the knowledge that I will impart to him tomorrow morning."

"All that matters is that you should be safe," Cara said. "I do not want to talk about it or even think about it. I only know that I heard them saying you must be killed, and I felt as if a dagger had been thrust into my . . . heart."

"Now you know, my darling, how I felt when I waited outside, fearing that at any moment those evil men might discover and perhaps torture you."

Cara gave a little cry, and the Marquis said:

"But you are safe, completely and absolutely safe, and never again, never, never, will I let you take part in anything so dangerous."

"I have no wish to do so," Cara said. "Because I love you, all I want to do is to please you and do what you want me to do."

The Maquis looked down at her with a tenderness in his eyes which no one had ever seen before.

"I love you just as you are," he said. "Actually, that is a very strange thing for me to say, but it is true."

"And I love you," Cara said. "When I said I hated men and was afraid of them, how could I have thought that I should love you until I feel that my whole body is throbbing with love? I want you to kiss me, and love me

until I can remember . . . nothing else but you and only
. . . you."

The way she spoke, with a little touch of passion in
her voice that had never been there before, made the
fire come into the Marquis's eyes.

He was intelligent enough to realise that Cara's
defiance and her hatred of men had come from the
treatment she had received from her uncle and the fact
that she had been alone and helpless in a world that was
very frightening.

But because she had so much character and spirit, it
had not crushed her as it might have done another
woman.

Instead, she had fought back, determined to sur-
vive, determined to be herself. Yet, even while she gave
hatred for hatred, she was craving for love.

Feeling that his own emotions rising within him
were so overwhelming, so irresistible, the Marquis
turned Cara's face up to his and, looking at her, said:

"What have you done to me, my beautiful one, to
make me feel like this? And what have I ever done to
deserve anybody so perfect and so adorable as you?"

"Do you really mean that?" Cara asked. "I wanted
you to admire me, although I did not understand that
what I really wanted was to be . . . loved. Now I am so
happy that I feel as if you are carrying me . . . up to the
sky and I can . . . touch the stars. There is only beauty
and music round us, . . . and nothing . . . horrid or
. . . cruel."

She gave a little shudder as she said the last word,
and the Marquis knew she was remembering how her
uncle had hit her and beat her.

"Forget him!" he said softly. "He is finished. After
tomorrow night he will be in the Tower, and if he does
not take his own life, he will be tried by his peers and
condemned to death!"

As he spoke he was quite certain in his own mind
that when the Earl learnt that the conspiracy had been

discovered and the rebels arrested, he would shoot himself.

There was no chance of his not being implicated. Thistlewood would undoubtedly betray him, and amongst his own servants, apart from the rebels, there were witnesses to his guilt.

Normally the Marquis would have felt satisfaction at the defeat of his enemy, but now he was thinking primarily of Cara and that the horror the Earl had brought into her life would gradually fade from her mind.

Enveloped by his love and the love she had for him, she would forget, and there would only be the glory and joy of being together.

As if she knew what he was thinking, Cara said softly:

"I love you! How can I make you . . . realise how much I love you . . . and that . . . nothing else in the world . . . matters except . . . you?"

"That is what I want you to say," the Marquis answered, "and go on saying it not once but a thousand times."

He turned round in bed so that he could look down at her and thought that with her eyes brilliant with happiness filling her small face, he had never seen real beauty before.

Then the warmth and softness of her body and her fingers holding tightly on to him as if she was afraid she might lose him made the Marquis feel the flames rising from the fire she had lit within him.

He told himself that he must be very gentle because Cara was so precious, and while he would awaken her to the love which raged within him like an inferno, he would do so slowly and tenderly, so that she responded to it like a flower opening its petals a little more each day.

Because he was a very experienced lover, he had

already evoked in her a response which he felt, as Cara had, lifted him into the sky.

But he knew this was only the beginning of the ecstasy they could arouse in each other, which would grow and grow.

He knew that never in his numerous love-affairs had he ever had to teach anybody so young or so exquisite, and it was in fact the most exciting thing he had ever experienced in his life.

When he looked at Cara he knew that all the women who had come and gone, who had tried to hold his attention and failed, had been but a shadow of the reality he felt now.

Like pale ghosts they had already disappeared into the past, and he would never think of them again.

His instinct, which Cara had recognised joined with hers, told him that he had found the real love which all men seek with the woman who is the other part of themselves.

He thought that with Cara's courage and resilience, and with her personality, which was very unusual in anybody so young, she was in fact the complement to his own character that he would have looked for if he had understood his need of her as fully as he did now.

He felt not only a desire for her rising steadily and insistently, but also a deep, mysterious gratitude to the fate that had brought him the El Dorado that all men seek.

As if she was a little puzzled by his silence and the way he was looking at her, Cara asked:

"Are you . . . thinking of . . . me?"

"Only of you, my lovely one. You fill my eyes, my mind, my heart, and my soul—if I have one."

"That is what I wanted you to say, because it is the same way that I . . . love you."

Then she said very softly:

"Will you tell me everything you want me to do so that I will not disappoint you? Because I love you, I want to be perfect, absolutely perfect, but it will be difficult if you do not help me."

The Marquis drew in his breath.

"You just have to be you, my darling. It is as easy as that."

She smiled so that he saw her dimples and an irresistible twinkle in her eyes as she answered:

"Have I really captured the elusive Marquis? I thought it was an impossibility!"

"I thought it was, too," the Marquis admitted, "but I have also caught you, and I promise you there is no escape. You will never run away and I will never, never lose you."

"Make me . . . sure of that," Cara whispered. "Love me, Ivo, and make me sure, please . . . please I want . . . you to love . . . me."

As she spoke she moved closer to him, and the Marquis felt as if he could feel the little flame that had awakened within her flickering against his body.

Then as his arms went round her and his heart beat against hers, he knew they were no longer two people but one. They were flying into the sky and leaving behind everything that was sordid, evil, and cruel, and nothing would ever hurt them again.

ABOUT THE AUTHOR

BARBARA CARTLAND is the bestselling authoress in the world, according to the *Guinness Book of World Records*. She has sold over 200 million books and has beaten the world record for five years running, last year with 24 and the previous years with 24, 20, and 23.

She is also an historian, playwright, lecturer, political speaker and television personality, and has now written over 320 books.

She has also had many historical works published and has written four autobiographies as well as the biographies of her mother and that of her brother, Ronald Cartland, who was the first Member of Parliament to be killed in the last war. This book has a preface by Sir Winston Churchill and has just been republished with an introduction by Sir Arthur Bryant.

Love at the Helm, a novel written with the help and inspiration of the late Earl Mountbatten of Burma. Uncle of His Royal Highness Prince Philip, is being sold for the Mountbatten Memorial Trust.

In 1978, Miss Cartland sang an Album of Love Songs with the Royal Philharmonic Orchestra.

She is unique in that she was #1 and #2 in the Dalton List of Bestsellers, and one week had four books in the top twenty.

In private life Barbara Cartland, who is a Dame of the Order of St. John of Jerusalem, Chairman of the St. John Council in Hertfordshire and Deputy President of the St. John Ambulance Brigade, has also fought for better conditions and salaries for midwives and nurses.

As President of the Royal College of Midwives (Hertfordshire Branch) she has been invested with the first badge of Office ever given in Great Britain, which was subscribed to by the midwives themselves.

Barbara Cartland is deeply interested in vitamin therapy and is president of the British National Association for Health. Her book, *The Magic of Honey*, has sold throughout the world and is translated into many languages.

She has a magazine, "Barbara Cartland's World of Romance," now being published in the USA.

Barbara Cartland

The world's bestselling author of romantic fiction. Her stories are always captivating tales of intrigue, adventure and love.

☐ 20935	LOVE'S HOUR	$2.50
☐ 22611	CAUGHT BY LOVE	$2.25
☐ 22712	KNEEL FOR MERCY	$1.95
☐ 22711	THE CALL OF THE HIGHLANDS	$1.95
☐ 22611	CAUGHT BY LOVE	$1.95
☐ 22513	MUSIC FROM THE HEART	$1.95
☐ 20815	MOMENTS OF LOVE	$1.95
☐ 20948	LOVE RULES	$1.95
☐ 20747	LIES FOR LOVE	$1.95
☐ 20746	THE VIBRATIONS OF LOVE	$1.95
☐ 20574	LOOKING FOR LOVE	$1.95
☐ 20235	LOVE WINS	$1.95
☐ 20505	SECRET HARBOUR	$1.95
☐ 20234	SHAFT OF SUNLIGHT	$1.95
☐ 20014	GIFT OF THE GODS	$1.95
☐ 20126	AN INNOCENT IN RUSSIA	$1.95
☐ 20013	RIVER OF LOVE	$1.95
☐ 22822	WISH FOR LOVE	$2.25
☐ 22876	MISSION TO MONTE CARLO	$2.25
☐ 14902	WINGED MAGIC	$1.95
☐ 14922	A PORTRAIT OF LOVE	$1.95

Buy them at your local bookstore or use this handy coupon for ordering: